DR WHO AND THE
ARMAGEDDON FACTOR

Also available in the Target series:

DR WHO AND THE ARMAGEDDON FACTOR

Based on the BBC television serial by Bob Baker and Dave Martin by arrangement with the British Broadcasting Corporation

TERRANCE DICKS

published by
the paperback division of
W. H. Allen & Co. Ltd

A Target Book
Published in 1980
by the Paperback Division of W. H. Allen & Co. Ltd.
A Howard & Wyndham Company
44 Hill Street, London W1X 8LB

Printed in Great Britain by
Richard Clay (The Chaucer Press) Ltd,
Bungay, Suffolk

ISBN 0 426 20103 5

1

The Vanishing Planet

'Atrios!' said the Doctor. 'Do you know, I've never been to Atrios.'

Romana looked up from the TARDIS's control console. 'What about Zeos?'

'Where?'

'Zeos, its twin. "Atrios and Zeos are twin planets at the edge of the helical galaxy." Didn't they teach you anything at the Academy?'

'But we're not going to Zeos!' protested the Doctor.

'No, we're going to Atrios.'

'Well, what are we hanging about for? Why don't you get on with it?'

Romana's hands moved skilfully over the controls. 'Atrios, here we come! I wonder what it's like?'

The wandering Time Lord known as the Doctor and Romana his Time Lady companion, were nearing the end of a long and dangerous quest. Some time ago, the White Guardian, one of the most powerful beings in the cosmos had set them a vital task—to find and reassemble the six fragments of the Key to Time. Long ago the Key had been divided, and the segments scattered to the far corners of the cosmos.

Now the Key was needed again, to enable the White Guardian to correct a state of temporal imbalance which was threatening the universe, and frustrate the schemes of the evil Black Guardian.

The Doctor's task was complicated by the fact that the segments of the Key had a number of mysterious powers, including that of transmutation. They could take on the shape of anything from a pendant to a planet. To aid them in their search, the Doctor and Romana had been given the Tracer, a slender wand-like device which could be plugged into the TARDIS console. The Tracer could lead them to the planet on which a segment of the Key was located. Unplugged, it could be used as a detector, once the planet had been reached. Finally, it had the power to make the segment assume its proper form—a large, irregularly-shaped chunk of crystal.

After many dangerous adventures, five segments were now in the Doctor's possession, merged together to form one large crystal. Only the sixth and final segment remained to be found. According to the Tracer, that final segment was somewhere on Atrios.

Some time later, Romana looked up from the console. 'We're almost there, Doctor. Time to materialise.'

The Doctor moved her aside. 'Right. I'll handle this bit myself.' His hands flicked over the controls, and the TARDIS left the space/time continuum, appearing in normal space in the incongruous shape of a police box. 'I've put us in a parking orbit around Atrios. Let's take a look.'

The Doctor switched on the scanner. The screen was blank. 'That's very odd! Wouldn't you say that was very odd, Romana?'

'That's very odd,' said Romana obediently. 'Better re-check your co-ordinates, Doctor.'

'I fed in the ones you gave me. Are you sure they were correct?'

'*Quite* sure, Doctor. Your TARDIS must have gone astray again.'

'Give me another reading.'

Romana moved round to the part of the console that held the Tracer. 'Zero, zero, four, zero, eight, zero, one zero.'

'What a lot of zeros!' The Doctor operated the controls again. The TARDIS dematerialised almost immediately. He looked at the scanner. A tiny reddish-brown sphere was just visible in the centre of the screen. 'There's *something* anyway!'

Romana checked the navigational readings. 'That's Atrios all right, but it's millions of miles away. And where's the twin planet, Zeos? There's no sign of it.'

'You know what I think?' asked the Doctor solemnly. 'I think something's gone wrong. Only some very powerful force could confuse the TARDIS's navigational circuits like that. It's as if someone doesn't want us to find Atrios.'

'The Black Guardian?'

'Well, it *could* just be coincidence ...'

'I wouldn't like to bet on it,' said Romana grimly.

'Nor would I. But there's only one way to find out what's going on.'

'I know ... Why don't you take us in on manual, Doctor?'

'You know what? I think I'll take us in on manual —with considerable circumspection ...'

The space pilot was impossibly handsome, the nurse in his arms a vision of loveliness.

'Don't go, my love,' she begged. 'You'll be killed! I love you!'

'And I love you. But there is a greater love than ours, and out there my friends are dying for it. Dying, so that Atrios may live! You must be strong, my love, till victory is won, evil vanquished, peace restored. Only then can we love again.' He kissed her tenderly. 'Now I must go. Kiss the children for me. Tell them that one day their daddy will come home again.'

Martial music swelled to a climax; the young lovers faded from the screen, to be replaced by the stylised eagle that was the symbol of Atrios.

The music merged with the distant scream of an air raid siren and the thud of an explosion.

Irritably the Marshal flicked off the video screen. Sentimental rubbish, but no doubt it served to hearten the more simple-minded citizens of Atrios for the continuing struggle. Those of them who were still alive ...

The Marshal of Atrios gazed gloomily around his War Room. It was an enormous circular chamber with thick metal walls decorated in green and black. Underground, of course. Everything on Atrios was underground now, and had been for years. The high radiation levels made life on most of the surface impossible.

The War Room was a giant communications centre, with instrument consoles and computer terminals and read-out screens everywhere. It was from here that the unending war with Zeos was directed. All over the room technicians were working feverishly. Black-helmeted, black uniformed guards stood at the doors.

Major Shapp, the Marshal's aide and assistant, was studying the read-out screen on the main battle computer. He was a rather stout and intensely serious young man, and his round face looked somehow incongruous above the high collar of his plain black uniform.

The Marshal himself was a far more imposing figure. Tall and broad shouldered, straight-backed with iron-grey hair, he wore a magnificent scarlet tunic with gold epaulettes, the eagle of Atrios emblazoned in silver on the breast. His stern face was rugged and handsome, his voice deep and commanding.

A flood of reports was coming in from the missile sites that studded the planetary surface. 'Area six, obliterated ... Section seven, heavy damage ... District ten, no contact. Level fourteen, holding and functional ... Area three, no contact. Heavy casualties on all upper levels ...'

As the reports came in, Shapp punched them into the main computer, which was constantly revising and up-dating the grid map on the main display screen.

Beside Shapp, stood a slender purple-gowned figure, the gold circlet of royalty on her golden hair. This was the Princess Astra, in theory the ruler of the planet. In reality, Atrios had been so long at war that all real power was now in the hands of the military establishment—which meant the Marshal.

He crossed the War Room to stand between them, his uniformed bulk towering over them both. 'What news of our counter-attack, Shapp?'

'None, Marshal. Our space fleet is still trying to locate the target.'

'The target, Major Shapp, is the planet Zeos! Isn't it big enough for them?'

'The navigational systems are being blocked. The Zeons must be using some new screening device. The whole spacefleet's flying blind.'

'Is it? Or have they all turned cowards? I want that attack pressed home, Shapp, before the Zeons smash our planet to pieces. *Is that clear?*'

Shapp bowed his head. 'Yes, sir.'

An urgent voice crackled from one of the loud-speakers. 'Direct hit reported on hospital complex. Wards seven to ten destroyed.'

Princess Astra caught her breath in horror. 'I must go there at once.'

She headed for the door but a guard barred her way. 'I'm sorry, Your Highness. You can't leave here without an escort—Marshal's orders.'

Astra swung round on the Marshal. 'I insist on going to the hospital immediately.'

He shook his head. 'Too dangerous.'

'But they've been hit!'

'So has everywhere else, Your Highness. We happen to be under nuclear attack.'

Princess Astra glared up at him furiously. 'How much longer must this futile war go on? Atrios is being destroyed around us. We must negotiate before it's too late. We must have peace!'

'You don't beg for peace, Princess. You win it. Our counter-attack is already under way. When it has succeeded, victory will be within our grasp. Then we shall have peace.'

'But don't you understand? If the war goes on we shall all be wiped out, Zeons and Atrians alike.'

'I understand only my duty, Princess—which is to bring this war to a successful conclusion.' The Marshal paused. '*Your* duty is to comfort and inspire your people.'

'Then let me go to the hospital and do it. I can do no good here.'

The Marshal sighed, wondering, not for the first time how so much obstinacy could be packed into one slim body. 'What's the situation, Shapp. Is the raid over?'

'Yes sir, at least for the moment.'

'Very well. Princess Astra, one of my guards will escort you to the hospital. No doubt Chief-Surgeon Merak is anxiously awaiting you.'

Princess Astra gave him a resentful look and swept from the room, a guard at her heels.

The Marshal went to the massive throne-like command chair which dominated the centre of the room. 'Set up the video-links, Shapp. I shall address the people.'

The hospital complex looked like a scene from hell. The dead and dying were everywhere. Patients from the bombed-out wards had to be transferred to wards that had been overcrowded to begin with and were now full to bursting point. The bodies of the wounded were strewn along the corridors.

Chief-Surgeon Merak moved through the chaos, directing the efforts of the doctors, nurses and orderlies, trying to create some order in the chaos. He was a darkly handsome man in the black and red gown of a surgeon, still young and virile, though at the moment his face was lined with weariness. Merak was the son of one of the oldest families on Atrios, who had rejected high political office in favour of the life of a healer. He had been in love with Princess Astra since they were both children, and she with him, although the fact was known only to their closest friends.

Merak paused for a moment in the main ward examining a badly wounded pilot who lay in a coma on a mattress on the floor. The sudden move had worsened the man's condition and his pulse was failing.

A booming voice interrupted Merak's examination. 'Citizens of Atrios!'

Merak looked up. The video screen on the wall of the ward was functioning again, and it was filled with a giant close-up of the Marshal's face. 'Once more the hated forces of Zeos clamour at our gates. Once more they shall not pass. Be brave, my people. Be steadfast. Be strong!'

Merak's patient groaned suddenly and his head fell back. He was dead.

Merak shot an angry glance at the screen, where the Marshal was still mouthing inspiring platitudes, and signalled two orderlies to carry the body away.

He was about to move on, when a familiar voice called 'Surgeon Merak!'

Princess Astra had just entered the ward, her face white and angry. 'Why are brave men and women being left to lie in the corridors like rubbish?'

Merak gestured around him. Except for the central aisle, not an inch of floor-space was free. 'Because as Your Highness can see, the wards are full.' He rose and walked down the aisle towards her, studying the plastic indicator clipped to the breast of her gown. 'If Your Highness will excuse me, your rad-check is due for renewal. If you would come this way?' He led her to the little corner cubicle that served as his office, closing the door in the face of the suspicious guard. Once alone they embraced briefly, and then drew apart. Astra looked anxiously at Merak. 'Are you all right? When they told me the hospital had been hit ... I was so worried.'

Merak nodded wearily. 'I was lucky.'

Astra was close to tears. 'When will it end, Merak?'

'Have you been able to contact the Zeons?'

Merak and Astra were the leaders of an underground peace party, trying to end the war by negotiation.

Astra shook her head despairingly. 'None of our messages seem to get through.'

Merak frowned. 'Is it possible the transmissions are being jammed from this end?'

'No. That would mean the Marshal suspected us— and if he did, he'd have us arrested. I sent the last message myself. On the palace transmitter. There was no contact-signal, no bounce back—nothing! It's as if Zeos wasn't there!'

The rumble of a nearby explosion shook the room. The atomic bombardment had started again. Merak looked up. 'Zeos is there, all right.'

A voice from the doorway said, 'Forgive me, Your Highness but we are behind schedule.'

They turned. It was the guard.

Merak took a new rad-check from his desk, took off the one the Princess was wearing, and put the new one in its place. 'You really must be careful to keep your rad-check renewed, Princess,' he said severely.

Astra nodded coolly. 'Thank you, Surgeon Merak.' She turned and followed the guard from the room.

Merak watched her go, his face grim. They must make contact with Zeos—before their entire planet was destroyed.

2

Missile Strike

The Marshal sat slumped in his command chair, staring broodingly at the busy War Room. They were losing, he thought gloomily. Unless something happened soon ...

Shapp's voice aroused him from his reverie. 'Marshal, I think we're getting something. An unidentified object.'

The Marshal rose, and went over to the main radar section. A tiny blip was moving slowly across the main screen.

'It's a completely unknown signal profile, sir,' said Shapp excitedly. 'It's hardly moving at all.'

The Marshal slammed his fist down on the console. 'It's the Zeon secret weapon. The device that's interfering with our navigation. Keep tracking until it's within missile range. Destroy that—*thing* and we can still win! I'll show Princess Astra and her pacifist friends.'

The Marshal moved away from the radar section and went over to an alcove in a quiet corner of the War Room. There was a mirror in the rear wall of the alcove—a very strange mirror. It had an elaborately decorated metal border and its glass was so darkened that one seemed to stare through it rather than into it. The Marshal gazed at his shadowy reflection, and spoke, as if addressing someone else. 'She is beginning to panic, becoming a thorn in my flesh, an irritant. She could be useful to my enemies.' The Marshal paused, almost as if expecting a reply. Then he nodded slowly. 'Yes ... something tells me her usefulness is coming to an end.' He moved over to the communications area.

At the sound of the subdued bleep, Princess Astra's guard paused. 'Excuse me, Your Highness.' He lifted his wrist communicator to his ear. 'Yes, sir, she's with me now.' He paused. 'Yes, sir. Very good sir. I'll see to it immediately.' He turned to the Princess. 'New orders, Your Highness. Your visit to the children's ward has been cancelled, danger of subsidence. The children are being evacuated to K block. We're to go there now, so that you can meet them in their new quarters.'

'I thought K block was closed by radiation contamination.'

'That was some time ago, Your Highness, apparently it's clear now. This way please.'

'Very well.'

Their route led them into a wing that seemed completely deserted. The guard paused before an arched metal doorway. 'In here, Your Highness. The children are waiting for you.' He opened the door. There was darkness beyond the doorway, and no sound of children's voices.

Princess Astra hesitated, and the guard said, almost regretfully, 'You *must* go in, Your Highness. I have my orders.'

'I understand.' She went through the doorway, and the guard slammed and locked the door behind her. As he straightened up, a shadow fell across him.

The Marshal was standing over him, blaster in hand.

The guard came to attention. 'Your orders have been carried out, sir.'

'Excellent,' said the Marshal, and shot him down.

Princess Astra found herself in a long, dimly-lit, metal-walled room. It was completely empty, and the walls and floor were thick with dust. She spun round and tried the door. It was shut fast. There was a warning bleep from the rad-check in her lapel. Princess Astra looked down. The little device was pulsing steadily with light. It was the alarm signal. K block wasn't clear of radiation after all.

Romana looked up from her instrument-readings. 'Still no sign of Zeos, Doctor. But I'm getting a clear reading for Atrios, Radiation levels you wouldn't believe. Look!'

The Doctor looked. 'Good grief! You could fry eggs on the streets.'

'There must be a nuclear war going on down there!'

'Not necessarily.'

'What other explanation is there?'

'Maybe someone's holding a very large breakfast party! Why do you always assume the worst, Romana?'

'Because it usually happens!'

'Empirical poppycock! Where's your joy in life? Where's your optimism?'

'It opted out,' said Romana gloomily.

An inner door opened and a creature rather like a metal dog glided into the control room. This was K9, the Doctor's other companion. In appearance he was rather like a robot dog, but in reality he was a fully mobile self-powered computer, with defensive capabilities. The Doctor looked down at him. '*You* know what optimism means, don't you, K9?'

K9 whirred and clicked as he consulted his data banks. 'Optimism. Irrational belief, bordering on the insane, that everything will work out well.'

'Oh shut up, K9,' snapped the Doctor, none too pleased with this definition. 'Now listen, Romana, whenever you approach a new situation, you must always believe the best until you find out what's really going on. Then you can believe the worst!'

'But suppose it turns out not to be the worst after all?'

'Don't be ridiculous, it always does!' The Doctor rubbed his chin. 'Nuclear war, eh? It's always difficult walking into these situations, you never know who's fighting who.'

'Or why,' said Romana gloomily.

'Oh, I think we can guess why.'

'We can?'

The Doctor's face was grave. 'It's got to be something to do with what we're looking for, hasn't it? The sixth and most important segment of the Key to Time!'

The Marshal strode briskly into the War Room. 'All well, Shapp? What about our mystery object?'

'Still there, sir. It's not moving at all now. It could be on surveillance sir, monitoring and observing us.

'Is it within missile range yet?'

'Yes, sir.'

The Marshal rubbed his hands. 'Then it won't be spying on us much longer.' His voice hardened. 'Vaporise it, Shapp. Now!'

Romana was studying the scanner. 'Doctor, something seems to be approaching us from the planet surface.'

'Maybe it's a welcoming party. What do you make of it, K9?'

'Welcoming party negative. Object identified as ground-to-air missile. Nuclear warhead.'

'We'd better get out of here.'

'Wait,' said the Doctor. 'We'll dematerialise at the last moment, confuse the enemy. Link the Tracer into the guidance systems, Romana, I'd like to be near the segment when we land. The less time we spend on Atrios the better!'

'I quite agree!' Romana busied herself at the other side of the console.

The Doctor waited, his hand on the dematerialisation switch. 'Stand by, everyone. How long, K9?'

K9 began a countdown. 'Four ... three ... two ... one ...'

The Doctor threw the dematerialisation switch. 'Zero!'

*

19

Eyes fixed on the radar screen, the Marshal waited. He saw the missile track streak across the screen, towards the mysterious object. They touched—and object and missile disappeared.

'Got it! We got it! Well done Shapp, you've earned yourself a medal!'

Shapp looked up from his instrument readings. 'Thank you sir. But I don't really know ...'

'Don't know what?'

'If we got it.'

'I saw it with my own eyes, man!' The Marshal smashed one fist into his open palm. 'A direct hit. Beautiful. That's what war's all about.'

Shapp nodded slowly. 'Yes, sir. But the thing is ... I could swear the target disappeared just *before* impact.'

In a deserted corridor deep below the hospital complex there was a strange, wheezing groaning sound, and a square blue box appeared from nowhere.

After a moment, the TARDIS door opened, and the Doctor emerged winding his incredibly long scarf around his neck, and tugging on his broad-brimmed floppy hat. He looked round cautiously, and then beckoned behind him. Romana came out of the TARDIS. They were in a long, gloomy underground corridor, its walls cracked and peeling, its floor littered with rubble. 'I wonder how far down we are?'

The Doctor looked over his shoulder. 'K9, are you sulking in there? It's all right, you can come out now. No water, no swamps, no monsters. It's quite safe.'

K9 glided out of the TARDIS and swivelled to and

fro in a semi-circle, his sensors scanning the environment. From somewhere above them came the distant rumble of an explosion.

K9 cocked his head. 'Radiation levels indicate nuclear warfare in progress on planet surface.'

Romana shot a triumphant look at the Doctor. 'You see? How deep are we, K9?'

'Four hundred metres below planetary surface, Mistress.'

The Doctor whistled. 'Four hundred! The whole planet must be taking a pasting. If this is what it's like four hundred metres down, imagine what it must be like on the surface.'

'What about radiation levels?' asked Romana nervously.

K9 whirred and clicked. 'Radiation levels variable, but within Time Lord tolerances, no life-forms near at present. Recent corpse in immediate vicinity.'

K9 glided along the corridor and around a corner. The Doctor and Romana followed. Just around the corner, they saw the huddled body of a man in uniform lying at the foot of a heavy metal door.

The Doctor examined the body. 'You're right, K9. Poor chap hasn't been dead very long. Seems to have been shot at close range, and from the front—which suggests it was someone he knew. Just goes to show—you can't trust anybody these days!'

Romana shivered. 'I don't think I'm going to like this planet very much.'

'Nor me. Let's hurry up and find the sixth segment so that we can get away from here.'

'I couldn't agree more, Doctor.' Romana switched on the Tracer and moved it round in a semi-circle.

To her surprise the electronic beep led her straight to the metal door. 'It seems to be through there.'

The Doctor examined the door. 'Lead-shielded by the look of it.' He tried the handle. 'And locked. Now what does that suggest, Romana?'

'A high, radiation-zone?'

'Affirmative,' confirmed K9.

Thoughtfully the Doctor studied the door. 'What's in there, K9? Any sign of sentient life forms?'

K9 scanned the door. 'Regret lead shielding prevents effective analysis.'

'Well, whatever it is, it's guarded.' The Doctor looked down at the sprawled body. 'Or at least it was guarded. Perhaps the door's booby-trapped.'

Romana caught her breath. 'The Black Guardian?'

'It's a possibility. "Will you walk into my parlour, said the spider to the fly?" Do you think you could blast me a hole in that door, K9?'

'Affirmative, Master.'

'A very *small* hole to begin with, I think. You never know what's in there!'

K9 trundled forward, extruded the muzzle of his blaster and began to drill.

3

Kidnapped

Princess Astra sat huddled in a corner of the empty room, hands clasped around her knees, the gold circlet of royalty gleaming on her bowed head.

The rad-check on her lapel still pulsed faintly in the semi-darkness. According to its readings, the radiation level in the room wasn't quite as bad as she feared. It would be hours before she suffered any real harm. But then, thought Astra despairingly she looked like being here for hours—for days, weeks perhaps before anyone found her. It was simply a question of whether she died from radioactivity, or from hunger and thirst.

Suddenly she tensed. The metal walls muffled almost all sound—she had pounded and screamed at it for what seemed hours before giving up in despair. But hadn't she heard something just then—some faint sound?

She raised her tear-stained face, stared hopefully at the door and saw a tiny point of light!

The Marshal stared broodingly into his dark mirror.

He started as Shapp touched him deferentially on the shoulder. 'Never do that!'

Shapp jumped back. 'Sorry, sir.'

'I was thinking ... Well, what is it?'

'The alarm sensors in K block indicate a break-in attempt, sir. I thought I'd better tell you. I mean, why would anyone want to break *into* a high-rad zone?'

The Marshal scowled at him. 'All right, Shapp, I'll deal with this myself, understand? No one else is to be involved. No one. Oh, and find the traitor Merak and bring him to me!'

Fumbling for his blaster, the Marshal hurried from the room.

The door's lead shielding must have been mixed with some kind of strengthening alloy. It took K9 quite some time to drill even a small hole in it. At last the Doctor said, 'That's enough K9, move back will you? Go back down the corridor and keep watch.'

K9 retreated, and the Doctor knelt and put his eye to the hole. To his surprise he saw another eye looking back at him. The eye vanished to be replaced by a mouth, and a low voice whispered, 'Help me, whoever you are ...'

'Doctor!' called Romana.

The Doctor looked up. A bulky man in an elaborate military uniform was covering them with a blaster. 'Who are you?'

The Doctor got slowly to his feet. 'I'm the Doctor and this is Romana. Who are you?'

'The Marshal of Zeos. What are you doing here?'

'Well, we're travellers, actually, and we got lost. We've just stumbled across this poor chap here. I'm afraid he's dead.'

The Marshal looked down at the crumpled body of the guard. 'So I see. You'll both be shot for this.'

'We didn't kill him,' protested Romana. 'We found him like that.'

'You expect me to believe that? This way, both of you. Move!'

The Marshal gestured with his blaster and they moved off down the corridor.

K9 glided into the darkness of a side tunnel, and waited, hiding. When the Marshal and his captives had passed by, he emerged and moved cautiously after them.

Peering through the hole, Princess Astra sobbed, 'Help. Please help me.'

But there was no one to reply.

As K9 moved along the corridors, his sensors picked up the vibrations of fresh explosions. The bombardment of Zeos had started again. He was passing the corridor leading to the TARDIS when there was another explosion, very close this time. The whole corridor shuddered and part of the roof actually caved in. The way to the TARDIS was blocked.

K9 hesitated for a moment, decided to tackle one problem at a time, and glided after the Doctor.

The Doctor gazed interestedly around the War Room, observing the harried technicians at their innumerable consoles, the computer read-out screens continually pouring out statistics, the communications set up and the giant space radar screen. He sensed an atmosphere of tension and despair. Atrios was immersed in total war, a war it was losing.

The Marshal settled himself in his command chair and glared down at his captives. 'What were you doing outside that door?'

'I told you,' said the Doctor calmly. 'We're travellers, we got lost in the bombardment, and we thought that door might lead us to safety.'

'That door leads only to death.'

'Then in that case, you obviously saved our lives. I mean, I can see you're obviously someone terribly important. It's really very good of you to take the time to save our miserable lives, sir. Now, if we could just be on our way?'

'You are Zeon spies,' thundered the Marshal. 'Spies and saboteurs.'

The Doctor smiled disarmingly. 'Do we look like spies? I mean, spies are supposed to look sort of shabby, and inconspicuous aren't they?'

Shapp came forward. 'Surgeon Merak is here, sir.' He stared at the prisoners. 'Who are these people, sir?'

'These are the intruders, Shapp, the ones who were trying to break into K block.'

'But why, sir? Where are they from?'

'I intend to find that out Shapp—before I execute them.'

Merak was brought forward, flanked by guards. He was very angry. 'Marshal, I have patients waiting——'

'Let them wait! Do you know these people?'

Merak stared at the Doctor and Romana. 'No. Am I supposed to?'

'I think you do know them, Merak. They are Zeon spies and saboteurs.'

'What has that got to do with me?'

'Princess Astra is missing, Merak. She was last seen with you. Since then her bodyguard has been found dead and she has vanished.'

'Missing?' Merak was appalled. 'We've got to find her. You must organise a full scale search ...'

'Everything that can be done is already being done,' said the Marshal dismissively. 'Now you listen to me, Merak. I understand that you don't agree with my conduct of this war.'

'I don't agree with war—any war,' corrected Merak. 'Neither does Princess Astra.'

'Just so. And it's because of this attitude that you have been misled, for the noblest of motives of course, into co-operating with the enemy?'

'No, Marshal, you're wrong!'

'It would be wiser to admit everything. I arrested these two spies myself, standing over the body of the Princesses's escort. My theory is that she's gone over to Zeos—where you planned to join her!'

The Marshal glared down at Merak in mock-indignation. He knew of course that none of these accusations was true. But by branding Merak and Astra as traitors he could strengthen his own grip on the planet.

The Doctor felt it was time to intervene. 'That's nonsense, Marshal, we didn't kill the guard. We're not even armed. Not unless you count this!' He produced a whistle from his pocket and held it out.

The Marshal leaned forward. 'What's that?'

'Oh, just an old dog-whistle. Care for a blow?'

'Shapp!' growled the Marshal.

Shapp took the whistle from the Doctor and examined it intently. He set it to his lips and blew hard. Nothing happened. Shapp tossed the whistle back to the Doctor. 'It's useless, sir.'

The Marshal said menacingly. 'Don't play the fool with me Doctor. Now, why are you here?'

'Tourism?' suggested the Doctor hopefully.

'In the middle of a nuclear war?'

'Well, I run this little Time-travel agency, you see. Battlefields past and future. See how civilisations die, that sort of thing. Isn't that right, Romana?'

'Oh absolutely,' agreed Romana hurriedly. 'It's very educational.'

'For the last time. What are you doing here?'

'Well, if you must know, we were looking for a key.'

'Nonsense!' roared the Marshal. 'Everything you are telling me is a pack of lies. You are enemy agents, you have murdered one of my guards, you've abducted Princess Astra, no doubt with the help of Merak. Unless you confess, and divulge her whereabouts you will all three be executed as spies, *do you understand*?'

'Very clearly put, I thought,' said the Doctor politely. 'But I'm sorry, I don't think we can help you.'

Unseen by the guards, K9 appeared at the doorway.

'Is that your last word?'

The Doctor grinned. 'I sincerely hope not! Still, I think we've been here long enough.' His voice hardened. 'We tell you the truth, and you refuse to believe us. You accuse us of crimes we haven't committed and now you threaten to shoot us. I'm afraid it's all too much, especially after a long journey. Come along Romana.' The Doctor turned away.

'Stay where you are,' ordered the Marshal furiously. 'If you make just one move ...'

Suddenly the Doctor shouted, 'Lights out please, K9!'

K9 located the central power-box, blasted it with his laser-ray and the entire room was plunged into darkness and confusion.

The Doctor grabbed Romana's hand and pulled her to one side of the door. 'Guards!' yelled the Marshal. 'Stop them! Shoot them down!'

Guards poured into the War Room from the corridor, adding to the confusion. As they thundered in, the Doctor, Romana and K9 slipped out of the door, Merak close behind them. Merak had no idea who these strange intruders were, but he was pretty sure he'd be safer with them than with the Marshal.

Once they were out in the corridor the Doctor shouted, 'Come on, run!'

'Where to?' gasped Romana.

'Back to the TARDIS!'

The gold circlet seemed very heavy on Astra's forehead. She slipped it off, and put it on the dusty floor beside her, rubbing her aching forehead wearily. Her head fell back, her eyes closed and she slid away into unconsciousness.

Suddenly the already-faint lighting in the room seemed to dim still further. At the same time, a crack, a line of light appeared in the opposite wall. It grew wider, wider, until it revealed itself as the edge of a door. A hidden panel in the wall was sliding slowly open. A shadowy figure in a long black hooded cloak slipped through the opening and moved silently across the room. It lifted the sleeping Princess Astra, carried her across the room and through the opening. The door slid closed behind them.

The Doctor and his companions came tearing along the corridor turned a corner and skidded to a halt. An immense pile of rubble filled the corridor ahead of them.

The way to the TARDIS was blocked.

4

A Trap for K9

Romana stared indignantly at the rubble. 'What's happened? Where's the TARDIS?'

The Doctor shrugged. 'Buried somewhere under that lot I imagine.'

'Then we're trapped. There's no way out. The guards must be close behind us, they'll be here any minute.'

The Doctor seemed unperturbed. 'K9's guarding our rear. He'll hold them back.'

'Listen!' said Romana suddenly. 'Someone's coming!'

Footsteps were hurrying towards them. A moment later Merak peered cautiously around the corner. At the sight of the Doctor he gave a sigh of relief. 'I hoped it was you. Listen, where is she? Where's Princess Astra?'

'Who wants to know?'

'My name is Merak. The Princess Astra and I are betrothed.'

'Well, all I can tell you is, just before the Marshal arrested us I found *somebody*—and from the voice it was a young lady.'

'Where? Where is she?'

The Doctor led the way around the corner. 'Behind that metal door.'

Merak gave him an anguished look. 'But that leads to a high-rad zone. We must get her out.' He began hurling himself uselessly against the door.

The Doctor moved him aside. 'Just a minute.' He bent and peered through K9's peephole. 'Can't see anybody.' He put his lips to the hole. 'Hello! Anybody in there?' There was no reply.

K9 appeared around the corner.

'Hello boy,' called the Doctor. 'Any sign of our pursuers?'

'I was able to mislead them, Master. They are running the wrong way.'

'Well done. Now then, K9 we want this door open. But be careful. There may be a young lady on the other side, and we don't want her harmed.'

'Understood, Master.' K9 glided forward, activated his blaster, and began cutting a circle around the lock.

Merak looked on amazed. 'What is that thing?'

'Don't worry,' said Romana reassuringly. 'K9 won't hurt you. He's with us.'

'But who are you? Are you Zeons, as the Marshal said?'

'No, of course not,' said the Doctor briskly. 'Don't worry, we're friendly. Romana, keep an eye out behind us will you?'

Romana moved to the corner and the Doctor went on, 'Merak, why should the Marshal want to do away with the Princess?'

'What makes you think he's behind it?'

'Too many coincidences. He didn't even *believe* those charges he was making just now. It was all acting.'

'Astra and I were trying to contact the Zeons, to

try and make peace. If the Marshal knew ... He *wants* the war to go on. I knew I was in danger, but I thought Astra would be safe. The Marshal needs her support, her influence with the people.'

K9 completed his circle and the lock fell away. 'Ready, Master.'

Merak thrust his way past the Doctor, pushed open the door and went into the room.

It was empty.

The Doctor and Romana followed. Romana had the Tracer in her hand. She moved it about the room. 'Nothing here, Doctor.'

Merak picked up the gold circlet from the floor. 'Look. She *was* here!'

'Yes,' said the Doctor thoughtfully. He was studying a line of tracks in the dusty floor, tracks that led to an apparently solid wall.

K9 was whirring and clicking agitatedly. 'It is inadvisable to remain too long in this environment.'

'Right,' said the Doctor. 'Come on you two.'

Merak held back. 'I want to stay here. If she died here ...'

The Doctor pulled him from the room. 'People aren't dissolved by radiation, Merak, you know that. If Astra isn't here, then she's somewhere else.'

'Standing here worrying won't help her,' added Romana. 'Let's get out and look for her.'

Reluctantly Merak allowed himself to be led away.

The Doctor looked down at K9. 'The radiation in here won't harm you, K9. I want you to stay here on guard. Have a look at that back wall, I think there's a passage behind it. See what you can do with your scanner.'

'Affirmative, Master.'

As they came out into the corridor the Doctor said, 'Merak, do you know what's behind that room?'

'Just part of the recycling shaft as far as I know.'

'Recycling what?'

'Scrap, metal waste. It's all recycled for the war effort. Anything metal goes down that shaft to be re-processed in the furnaces. Why?'

'Oh, just general interest,' said the Doctor vaguely. 'Come on.'

'Where to?' asked Romana. 'Shall we try to clear the rubble from the TARDIS? I'll go and get K9?'

The Doctor shook his head. 'Not yet. Anyway, we won't find the segment by running away. And I want to discover exactly what the Marshal's up to.'

The Marshal at that particular moment was staring broodingly into his dark mirror. He looked up as Shapp came over to him. 'Well?'

'We've picked them up on security scan, sir, moving along the corridors. Merak's with them. They're coming back this way.'

'Have them picked up immediately. What about that machine of theirs, the thing that shot out the lights?'

'No sign of it at the moment, sir.'

The Marshal thought for a second. 'That machine —made of metal, wouldn't you say?'

'Presumably, sir.'

'Recycle it, Shapp. Locate it and turn it into scrap, do you understand?'

Shapp understood very well. The Marshal didn't

care for being made a fool of—especially by a machine.

He went over to the security scanner screen and began flicking up pictures. Most of the city complex was covered by a network of spy cameras, but it was impossible to monitor them all at once. Shapp began scanning the area around K block, flicking, punching up pictures of empty corridors, deserted rooms. Suddenly he looked up. 'I've got it sir. It's still in K block.'

'Then get rid of it Shapp!'

Shapp moved to the console which controlled the semi-automated recycling network that ran beneath the city. 'There's an access shaft in the room itself. If I can time things just right ...' His hands moved over the controls.

K9 had just decided that there was not only a compartment but an energy source behind the wall he was watching, when he sensed vibration from the one to his right. He wheeled round to investigate. Suddenly a hatchway slid open in front of him. Through it came a rattle and clank of moving machinery. K9 glided a little nearer—suddenly the floor beneath him dropped away and he shot forward through the hatchway.

He whizzed helplessly down a short steep shaft and shot out into empty air. There was a drop of a few feet and he landed with a thud, upside down on some metal surface.

Quickly he scanned his surroundings. He was on a long metal conveyor belt, clanking forward through semi-darkness. On either side of him were chunks of twisted metal, a ruined engine, hull plates of a shattered space ship, broken steel girders.

K9 gave himself a quick check, and was relieved to find that his circuits appeared undamaged. But he was still helpless. One of the few major faults in K9's design was that once tipped off-balance he found it almost impossible to right himself.

Helpless as a beetle on its back, K9 was carried forward by the clanking conveyor belt.

The temperature seemed to be rising.

'I've got the machine, sir. It's en route to the recycling furnaces now.'

'Excellent, Shapp,' said the Marshal absently. He was still staring into the dark mirror. 'When you find the others, see that they're treated correctly.'

'No softening up sir?'

'No. Not yet. I think I may have a use for them ...'

The Marshal relapsed into his trance.

As they walked along the corridor Romana was still wondering about the missing segment. According to the Tracer it had been very close in the room in K block. And since it obviously wasn't the circlet ... 'Merak, have you known Princess Astra for a long time?'

'All my life,' said Merak simply.

'Apart from the circlet is there anything else that's always with her. Something she carries, or wears?'

'Not that I know of ...'

They turned a corner and found themselves facing a patrol of guards.

The leader raised his blaster. 'Stop!'

'Certainly,' said the Doctor obligingly.

'The Marshal wants to see you.'

'How very convenient. As it happens I want to see him!'

The guards marched them away.

Back at the War Room, Shapp was waiting for them. 'Doctor, you come with me. You two, wait here.'

'Nice of you to invite us back,' said the Doctor chattily.

Shapp led him over to the Marshal who was standing gazing into the dark mirror apparently unaware of their presence. The Doctor watched him curiously. The Marshal seemed to be listening. Occasionally he nodded, and his lips moved, though no words could be heard.

The Doctor turned to Shapp. 'Is he all right?'

'Sssh, he's meditating.'

'Is he like this often?'

'When things aren't going well, he makes most of his decisions this way.'

'I'm not surprised things aren't going well, in that case. Standing in front of a mirror nodding and talking to yourself. First sign of meglomania you know. Look at him, standing there like a ventriloquist's dummy ...'

The Doctor's voice trailed away. Had he stumbled across the truth? For all his loudness and flamboyance there was something odd, off-key about the Marshal.

Was he a dummy, a puppet of some mysterious force?

Suddenly the Marshal swung round, advancing on the Doctor with a beaming smile. 'Welcome, my friend!'

The Doctor glanced round, wondering if the Marshal was addressing someone else. 'Friend? Last time we met you were going to have me shot!'

'A misunderstanding. I had forgotten that your coming had been foretold.' He sighed. 'The war, the endless war. It occupies my thoughts to the exclusion of all else. But now that you are here Doctor ... You are the one!'

'Am I really? Which one?'

The Marshal spoke with an air of total confidence. 'The one who will lead us to victory!'

'Oh, good. As long as there's no actual risk involved, you understand?'

The Marshal was off on another of his flights of oratory. 'We shall crush the hated Zeons in their tracks, wipe their presence from our skies, free this land, this world this Atrios this ...'

'Blessed plot?' suggested the Doctor helpfully.

'Exactly! Free this blessed plot from the evils of war and pestilence. And you, *you* shall give us our victory, Doctor.'

5

The Furnace

The Doctor stared at the Marshal in some amazement. 'I see. And what happens if I don't succeed?'

'The question does not arise.'

'I'm grateful for your confidence. I take it we're not under arrest any more?'

'My dear Doctor ...' The Marshal waved the idea away as utterly absurd.

Shapp came hurrying over to them. 'We've located the fleet, sir.'

'Then order immediate attack. Come, Doctor. You shall see it all.

The Marshal led the Doctor over to the main space radar screen which held two massed groups of tiny blips. 'There you are, Doctor, the mighty battle fleet of Atrios, and our Zeon foes. You shall see the weapons that are available to you, as the new architect of our victory.

'A dozen ships? Is that the mighty battle fleet of Atrios?'

'It would do my people no good to know the truth, Doctor. They live on hope, they have nothing else. Our factories are largely crippled, production almost at a standstill. But still we fight on, that is all that matters!'

'Is it? Why?'

'To win, of course. War is an expensive business—but worth it, as you shall see. Order the attack, Shapp!'

Shapp leaned forward. 'Base to Fleet. Commence attack!'

The Marshal added his voice. 'Attack! Attack! Attack!'

A line of four Atrian blips broke off from the main body and streaked towards the Zeon fleet.

Shapp flipped a relay and a confused babble of overlapping voices filled the War Room. 'Closing ... closing ... range four thirty. Hold on seven zero.' Report RDF and maintain attitude four three. Closing. We now have full combat state in all sectors.'

More and more blips broke off from the Atrian fleet. Zeon blips surged forward to meet them. Soon the big screen was a mass of swirling dots. Suddenly two blips coincided, and one of them disappeared in a burst of light.

'A hit, sir.' shouted Shapp. 'A hit, confirmed!'

Another Zeon blip disintegrated. 'And another!' shouted the Marshal.

There was a burst of cheering from the technicians.

Another blip disintegrated. 'That's one of ours, sir,' said Shapp.

There was another explosion. 'And that?' snapped the Marshal.

'Ours too sir.'

The battle went on, and it soon became apparent that blips representing Atrian ships were disappearing at a much faster rate than those of the Zeons.

Shapp looked anxiously at the Marshal. 'Shall I pull out, sir?'

'Never! Press home the attack!'

The battle raged on. One by one the Atrian ships were blasted from the screen. The Doctor looked on, his face bleak. It might have been some complicated electronic game—but he knew that each dot of light that vanished from the screen represented the deaths of a space fighter's crew, young men killed in a senseless war before their lives had really begun.

The Marshal's face was thunderous. 'What's the matter with them, Shapp? Why are they losing?'

'Inexperience, sir. They're brave but they're barely trained. The experienced crews were lost a long time ago.' There was a moment of silence.

'Pull them out,' ordered the Marshal.

Shapp leaned over the command mike. 'All units, disengage. All units, disengage.'

The screen went blank.

The Marshal turned to the Doctor. 'Three ships left, out of a once-proud battle fleet. You see now why we need your help? We must have a weapon that will sweep the aggressors from our skies once and for all. Can you provide it?'

'Oh, yes, I think so,' said the Doctor coolly.

'And the name of this weapon?'

'It's called peace.'

The Marshal laughed. 'Most amusing, Doctor. Peace! How can we have peace until we have the ultimate weapon.'

'Tell me, if you had this weapon, what would you do with it?'

'Use it of course, to make sure it worked.'

'Congratulations, Marshal,' said the Doctor ironically 'You have the true military mind.' He paused for a moment. 'Tell you what I'll do. You help me find the Princess Astra, and I'll knock you up a deterrent.'

The Marshal looked suspiciously at him. Then he beamed, and flung an arm across the Doctor's shoulders. 'I like you, Doctor, I really do. What will this weapon consist of?'

'Oh, a kind of parasol affair,' said the Doctor vaguely. 'An umbrella force-field, something no ship can penetrate.'

'Good! So we can attack, but they can't retaliate?'

'Well, not quite. It works both ways, you see. They can't get in, you can't get out.'

'Then how can we win? We must have *victory*!'

'There's always a snag—but I'll work on it. I'll need K9 of course.'

The Marshal looked at him. 'K9?'

'My mobile computer. Looks a bit like a robot dog.'

The Marshal swung round on Shapp. 'Well, you heard him.'

'It's probably too late, sir,' said Shapp desperately. 'It's well on the way to the furnace by now!'

The Doctor was horrified. 'Furnace? What furnace?'

Quickly Shapp explained what had been done with K9. 'He was sent for recycling, you see. We recycle all scrap.'

'Scrap!' said the Doctor savagely. 'Where is this furnace?'

'On the level just below us here—but it's too late!'

The Doctor grabbed Shapp's shoulders and shook him. 'Where is it man? Tell me how to get there—now!'

The recycling conveyor belt ran under most of the city complex, and luckily for K9 he had joined it at an early point of the cycle.

Carried on the belt he had travelled miles beneath the city. Every now and again there was a rattling and clanking as more scrap shot down onto the belt from the various access chutes, and once K9 himself was showered with metal debris.

Now it looked at if his luck was running out. The temperature had been rising steadily for some time, and there was a reddish glow in the air not far ahead. The conveyor-belt ran into a metal-walled room. He had reached the furnace.

The conveyor-belt ran across the room and straight into an open hatch beyond which there was nothing but a blazing glow of heat. At the edge of his vision, K9 could just see the chunks of scrap metal ahead of him disappearing one by one into the furnace. He could feel the searing heat beating against his casing.

There was only one thing he could do. 'Closing down,' said K9 faintly. 'All systems closing down.'

The door of the furnace room was flung open and the Doctor appeared.

He stood for a moment, eyes closed against the glare.

K9 was very near the end of the belt by now, within inches of the hatch.

Wrapping his scarf round his face, the Doctor plunged into the fiery glare around the furnace. He struggled forward, forcing his way through an almost-solid wall of heat ...

'Close down that furnace,' roared the Marshal.

Shapp was frantically busy at a control console.

'I already have, sir. But it takes weeks just to cool down ...'

'The Doctor must not die, Shapp. Not yet. And if he needs this K9 ...'

Shapp shook his head mournfully. 'If that thing's gone into the furnace, it'll be nothing but slag and clinker by now. Sorry, sir.'

'Sorry?' screamed the Marshal. 'Sorry?'

Almost choking with rage, he tugged at the collar of his tunic to loosen it.

Romana watched him curiously, wondering why danger to the Doctor should send the Marshal into such a fit of rage. As the Marshal pulled at his collar, she caught a glimpse of something at his neck—something like a tiny black cylinder.

She was trying to get a better look at it, when she heard a familiar voice from the doorway. 'Rather close for the time of year, don't you think?' She swung round, and there was the Doctor, leading K9 by the end of his scarf. The scarf was rather singed, along the edges, but the Doctor and K9 seemed perfectly unharmed.

'Doctor!' said Romana joyfully. 'Are you all right? And what about K9?'

The Doctor looked down at K9. 'All right now, old chap?'

'Affirmative.'

'You're not even singed!'

'Little trick I learned from the fire walkers of Bali,' said the Doctor modestly. 'They do this sort of thing all the time!'

The Marshal hurried forward and shook his hand. 'My apologies, Doctor to you and your—friend.'

'That's all right. I mean, we all make mistakes, don't we K9?'

'Negative, Master!'

Ignoring this, the Doctor went on, 'I gather you're not in favour of a two-way force-field Marshal. Well, if you're going in insist on our doing things your way ...'

'I am, Doctor.'

'I thought you might. Well, if we're going to set up a *one* way force-field, one which shuts the Zeons out but lets you through to attack them, we need to know our enemy, so to speak.'

'What do you mean?'

'It might be possible to construct a physchological barrier. Cheap, efficient, energy-saving, and it would stop the Zeons *wanting* to come here. Introduce an element of Atrophobia, you might say!'

Romana gave the Doctor a puzzled look. As far as she knew, he was talking utter nonsense. 'What a clever idea, Doctor,' she said loyally.

The Doctor went on, 'In order to do that I have to meet a Zeon. Find out how they think, brain patterns and so on. Isn't that right, Romana?'

'Oh, absolutely. There's no other way.'

The Doctor looked at the Marshal. 'You see? Romana agrees with me. Can you arrange it for me, Marshal?'

'No, Doctor.'

'It can be anyone, doesn't matter who. It doesn't even have to be someone intelligent, any old prisoner will do.'

'There are no prisoners, Doctor. Like us, the Zeons are sworn to destroy themselves rather than be captured. Death before dishonour!'

The Doctor sighed. 'Well, if you can't find us a Zeon, we shall have to think again.'

The Marshal gave him a warning glare. 'Time is running short, Doctor.'

'It is indeed,' agreed Romana. 'What about the Princess Astra—is there any news?'

'Intelligence sources sugguest she has been abducted by the Zeons. If she has ...' The Marshal waved his hand dismissively.

Shapp was over at the radar screen. 'Marshal, it's the Zeon fleet. They're closing in for another attack.'

The Marshal hurried over to the screen, and Romana turned to the Doctor. 'You know when you went down to the furnace, after K9? Well, the Marshal went almost berserk at the thought you might be killed.'

'How very considerate of him.'

'He kept on saying "the Doctor must not die—not yet!" And I saw something on his throat, some kind of cylinder.'

'A control device?'

'If the Marshal is a puppet—who's pulling the strings?'

'I wonder what's behind that mirror he's so fond of,' said the Doctor thoughtfully.

Merak had been hovering in the background for

some time, uncertain of his position. The Doctor's elevation from suspected spy to saviour of Atrios seemed to mean Merak was innocent by association, at least for the moment. It seemed wiser to lay low. Now he couldn't keep silent any longer. 'What's the use of all this? Questions, questions, questions, and never any answers. We're no closer to finding Astra or what you two are looking for either—well are we?'

'We may be closer to finding Astra than we realise,' said the Doctor mysteriously. 'What worries me is perhaps we're *supposed* to find her?'

'A trap?'

The Doctor nodded. 'Who's pulling the wool over who's eyes? Are we falling for the Marshal's bluff, or is he falling for ours.'

'Look,' said Merak desperately. 'Just tell me where you think Astra is and let me look for her. You can get on with looking for whatever you're after.'

'I'm prettty sure Princess Astra is on Zeos,' said the Doctor slowly. 'What I'd like to know is—why?'

Romana said, 'But no one seems to be able to find Zeos.'

The Doctor smiled ruefully. 'Oh, Zeos is there all right. We just can't see it.'

'Why not?'

He held his hand just in front of her eyes. 'Can you see me now?'

'Of course not, your hand's in the way.'

'Exactly!'

'You think there's something between us and Zeos? Then why can't we see the something?'

'Maybe it absorbs light and energy. Maybe its particularly well camouflaged. It could be something very small, or very large, but whatever it is, it's there!'

'How can you be so sure?' demanded Romana.

'How could Christopher Columbus be sure. I just know that's all.'

'Maybe that's why Astra couldn't get any signal back from Zeos,' suggested Merak. 'We've got to *do* something, Doctor. Where can we start?'

The Doctor nodded at the Marshal's wall mirror, 'By finding out what lies behind that mirror. There must be an entrance somewhere. Come on, K9, we've got some sums to do.'

The Doctor led K9 to a quiet corner of the War Room, and knelt down beside him.

Merak and Romana slipped quietly away. On his way out Merak helped himself to a tool-kit from a maintenance locker in the corner of the room.

6

Behind the Mirror

On the giant space radar screen the Zeon battle fleet was moving inexorably towards Atrios.

'Call up reinforcements,' ordered the Marshal.

'Their are none, sir,' said Shapp flatly. 'We've thrown everything we have at them, and still they keep coming.'

'This could be the last battle ...' The Marshal looked round. 'Where's the Doctor?'

He spotted the Doctor and K9 in their corner and marched over to them. 'Doctor, I *must* have that forcefield.' The rumble of a distant explosion shook the War Room. 'We're being obliterated, and we've nothing left to fight with. You're our last hope.'

'It's a problem of power,' said the Doctor thoughtfully.

'I'll give you absolute energy priority, everything you need.'

'I'm afraid you haven't got it. K9's just worked it out, haven't you K9?'

'Affirmative. To produce the energy to power a forcefield capable of protecting the entire planet, you would have to consume the whole of Atrios.'

'Which rather defeats the object,' the Doctor pointed out. Since you wouldn't have a planet to live on any more. You remember I mentioned a psychological deterrent, a barrier no Zeon could cross?'

'You said you would need Zeon prisoners to experiment on—and there are no Zeons.'

'There are on Zeos.'

'What exactly are you proposing, Doctor?'

'To go to Zeos, pick up a Zeon—and bring back Princess Astra—if she's there.'

Suddenly a technician called, 'We're picking up a video transmission, sir. From Zeos!'

They hurried across to a monitor and saw Princess Astra's face on the screen. 'People of Atrios! Lay down your arms! The Zeons have taken me captive and they swear to destroy Atrios unless you surrender now. If you love me, my people, save yourselves. Hand over the Marshal and—'

Hurriedly the Marshal lunged forward and switched off the monitor. He looked at the Doctor, his face pale. 'This psychological barrier of yours, Doctor—it would give us a breathing space?'

'It would give you time to save your neck yes.'

The Marshal glared angrily at him, and then controlled himself. 'You may go to Zeos, Doctor. There is a way ...'

Merak led Romana along a dark, cramped service tunnel. 'Should be just about here, I think, unless I've lost my sense of direction.' Merak produced tools from his pocket and began unscrewing a metal panel from the wall.

Romana watched impatiently; as soon as the panel came free she helped him to lift it down. Merak climbed through the gap, and Romana followed him.

They found themselves in a kind of secret chamber. It was very small, and there seemed to be a dimly lit window on the far side. Romana peered through it, and found herself looking at the Marshal. Behind him she could see the familiar bustle of the War Room. They were on the other side of the Marshal's two-way mirror. There was only one object in the room, a tall pedestal on which stood a gleaming crystal skull. Somehow it filled Romana with foreboding. It seemed to give out dark waves of evil.

Merak stared at the skull in astonishment. 'What is it?'

'Ssssh!' commanded Romana.

The Marshal was speaking, his voice low and urgent. 'It is done. The Time Lord suspects nothing. I have sent him to the transmat point in K block, where your servants are waiting.'

Romana caught her breath. 'Time Lord?' she thought. 'How does he know the Doctor is a Time Lord?'

The Marshal was still whispering. 'My Lord, once you have the secrets of Time please let me have my victory. I beg you. I have waited so long ...'

Romana was already climbing back through the gap. 'Come on Merak, we must find the Doctor and warn him.'

Hands in pockets, the Doctor strode through the gloomy corridors of K block, K9 at his heels. He was deep in thought. 'I've got a feeling I'm missing out on something, K9. Why should the Marshal, the leader of the war against Zeos, be the only one to know of a transmat link to the enemy planet? And why tell me about it if he does?'

He paused at the still-open door of the room from which Princess Astra had vanished. 'One of us, is being extremely stupid, K9!'

'Affirmative, Master!'

The Doctor walked into the darkened room. It was as bare and empty as when he had last seen it, silent, deserted, everything covered with dust. He crossed to the far wall and stood waiting at the point at which Astra's tracks disappeared.

Suddenly a section of wall slid open. Behind it was a dimly lit compartment with gleaming walls of some ornately-patterned, silvery metal. It looked not unlike a rather superior lift.

The Doctor drew a deep breath. 'Well, goodbye, K9. See you soon—I hope!'

He stepped inside.

Romana rushed into the room. 'No, Doctor, it's a trap!'

She was just in time to see two hooded skull-faced figures spring from the corners of the compartment and bear the Doctor to the ground.

The panel closed.

The Doctor struggled wildly for a moment. His opponents felt like living skeletons, but they were immensely strong.

A needle-sharp point pricked his thoat, and everything went black.

7

The Shadow

Merak came hurrying into the room just in time to see what happened. 'What are they doing in there?'

'Going to Zeos, I imagine.'

'How can they? It's a room.'

Romana shook her head. 'Oh no it isn't. It's a transmat point. Short for particle matter transmission. I'll explain it some time when we've got a couple of weeks to spare.'

'Those creatures we saw were they Zeons?'

'I suppose so. Now they've got Astra *and* the Doctor!' Romana headed for the door. 'Come on you two—we shall have to use the TARDIS.'

Romana led Merak and K9 to the rubble-blocked corridor in which they'd left the TARDIS. 'It's somewhere behind that lot, K9. Can you blast a way through to it?'

K9 scanned the pile of rubble, but made no attempt to fire.

'Hurry up K9. What's the matter?'

'Haste unnecessary, Mistress. Sensors indicate that TARDIS is missing.'

'Missing?'

'Affirmative.'

Romana looked at him in dismay.

*

The Marshal was still talking to the black mirror. 'You promised, My Lord. You promised me victory.'

In the hidden room behind the mirror the crystal skull glowed brightly. A voice came from it, a husky echoing voice filled with sardonic amusement. 'The war has served its purpose, as you have served yours. Now I have the Time Lord, there will be no more attacks from Zeos. Make of that what you will, Marshal.' The glow from the skull faded and the voice died away.

The Marshal heard only what he wanted to hear. 'No more attacks ... then I can still win! I can achieve a great victory, a *personal* victory. I shall lead the assault myself ...'

There was a murmur of astonishment from the technicians at the radar screen. Shapp hurried over. 'Marshal, the Zeon fleet—it's gone! They had us at their mercy, then they just disappeared!'

The Marshal gave a triumphant smile. 'We have exhausted them, Shapp. I shall lead the attack myself.'

The Doctor awoke in darkness, a circle of hooded skull-faced figures all around him. He seemed to feel something metallic at his throat. In front of him was a diamond-shaped cage made from bars of gleaming metal.

A voice said, 'Welcome, Doctor!'

The Doctor looked up. The speaker was standing a little apart from the others. At first glance he looked not unlike them. He too was black-robed with a face like a living skull. But the robes were of some rich

54

velvety material, and a collar of jewels blazed at his throat. Even without these symbols of authority, it would have been evident that this was the ruler of the sinister group. He had an aura of tremendous power and authority, and seemed to radiate darkness, so that light dimmed wherever he moved.

The voice was deep and husky at the same time, with a note of sardonic malice. It seemed to echo, as if coming from the depths of a tomb. 'I warn you, Doctor, you are completely in my power.'

The Doctor could feel the metal device at his throat, endeavouring to control his mind. He resisted it, reached up, and plucked the device from his throat. 'Oh really? Because of this?' He tossed the little cylinder aside.

A grimace of anger twisted the skull-like face. 'Seize him!'

Hooded figures thrust the Doctor into the diamond-shaped cage, fastening the locking bars.

The figure spoke again. 'I repeat Doctor, you are in my power. *Do you hear me?*'

Light crackled about the cage and a flood of agony swept through every nerve and sinew in the Doctor's body. The pain receded and the Doctor gasped. 'I hear you. Who are you?'

'I am the Shadow, Doctor. Your adversary, shall we say? It is not important. Listen carefully, Doctor. If you lie, there will be more pain. You came in search of a Key, the Key to Time, as it is called?'

'Yes.'

'You are already in possession of certain elements of this Key?'

'No.'

Sparks crackled about the cage and the Doctor gave a gasp of agony.

'I warned you,' said the voice. 'These elements—where are they?'

'Lost ...' muttered the Doctor. 'They're lost.'

'Open your eyes, Doctor.'

The Doctor obeyed. The darkness receded from the far corner of the room, to reveal the familiar square blue shape of the TARDIS.

The hateful voice said, 'Are they in there, Doctor?'

More light, more pain. 'Yes!'

'You will open it?'

'Yes.'

'Release him.'

The hooded figures unbarred the cage, and the Doctor fell unconscious to the floor.

Romana and Merak stood outside the transmat cubicle, watching as K9 played a finely concentrated laser-beam around the area of the lock.

Romana said impatiently, 'Please, hurry K9.'

'The locking mechanism is complex, Mistress, and I do not wish to damage the transmat. It will take time.'

'Listen,' said Merak suddenly. 'The bombing seems to have stopped. The Zeons must know we're done for. I wonder why they're bothering to take prisoners. First Astra, now the Doctor.'

'Because that's what this whole war has been leading up to.' Romana did her best to explain. 'The Doctor and I are looking for something called the Key to Time. Whoever holds it controls the balance of forces throughout space and time.'

Merak looked incredulously at her. 'Why do you want it? What will you do with it?'

'I can't tell you—but I assure you we don't want it for ourselves, and it will be used for good, not evil. The Key has been split into six segments, and they've been disguised and scattered throughout the universe. So far we've found five of them.'

'What has all this got to do with Astra?'

'She seems to be involved with the sixth piece in some way. Either she's carrying it, or she knows where it is.' Romana produced the Tracer. 'This is keyed to the segments of the Key to Time, but it seems to respond to Astra as well. So it can tell us the direction she's gone—and how close she is.'

Suddenly the door to the transmat slid open. 'Ready, Mistress,' said K9 proudly.

'Well done, K9.'

Abruptly Merak snatched the Tracer from Romana's hand, gave her a shove and leaped through the transmat door. 'Sorry, Romana,' he called—and the door slid closed.

The Doctor recovered consciousness for the second time to find himself lying on the floor outside the TARDIS. He got slowly to his feet, ignoring the Shadow and his black-robed servants and patted the TARDIS affectionately. 'Well, well, what are you doing here?' He looked at the Shadow. 'Correct me if I'm wrong, but this is Zeos, isn't it?'

'Do not waste my time, Doctor. Open the TARDIS and bring me the segments of the Key.'

The Doctor said amiably. 'Interested in time pieces are you? Chronostatics, horogenesis, that sort of thing?'

'You are not dealing with a fool, Doctor!'

'Oh, yes I am.' The Doctor examined the area around the TARDIS lock. 'Sorry to disillusion you, old chap. But you've obviously tried breaking and entering and failed. The TARDIS is covered in ADMs—automatic defence mechanisms. Very clever really.'

At a gesture from the Shadow, his servants produced blasters from beneath their robes. 'Bring me the first five segments of the Key to Time, Doctor, or I shall destroy you, *now!*'

'Do that and you'll never get in,' said the Doctor cheerfully. 'By the way, I take it you do know where the sixth segment is?'

'Destroy him,' snarled the Shadow.

The hooded figures raised their blasters.

The Doctor stepped back, raising his hands placatingly. 'There must be some civilised solution to all this.'

'Give me the five segments to the Key to Time.'

'I wish I could help you old chap. You see the segments are in a limbo safe, and the only way to open it is with the sixth piece. So if you'd like to let me have it, I'll be happy to go in and get them for you.'

The Shadow laughed. 'And do you think I would trust you, Doctor?'

'Not really—and I certainly don't trust you. Bit of an impasse, isn't it?'

There was a long pause before the Shadow spoke

again. 'I have waited so long, Doctor, that even another thousand years would be nothing to me. But
for you ... I have watched you in your jackdaw
meanderings. I know you, and I know there is no
patience in your nature.'

'You may be right. Fools rush in, you know.'

'Exactly.' The Shadow waved his hand, and his
servants faded away into blackness. 'I shall leave you,
Doctor, leave you to make your own mistakes. And
when you do—I shall be waiting!'

Suddenly the room-lights brightened. The Doctor
blinked and looked around him.

The Shadow and his servants had disappeared.

8

Lost on Zeos

The Doctor wasn't particularly surprised. There was something, odd, alien about the Shadow and his followers, as though they didn't really belong in this universe at all. They were real and yet not-real at the same time. The Doctor guessed that they came from some other, dark dimension, creatures of evil summoned up by the Black Guardian to aid him in his sinister schemes.

The TARDIS was still there, and instinctively the Doctor headed towards it. Then he checked himself. 'No, no, not yet, may as well have a look round. I might even find the sixth segment!'

He left the room and found himself in a long brightly-lit corridor, lined with supporting pillars. The walls were patterned in a pleasant shade of orange, very different from the grim blacks and greens of Atrios. The air was fresh and warm. The Doctor looked around. Other corridors branched off to the left and right. Choosing one more or less at random, the Doctor set off.

Not far away, Merak stumbled out of the transmat cubicle and found himself in a very similar corridor. He held up the Tracer, but no signal came. Merak raised his voice. 'Astra! Can you hear me? Astra, it's me!' His voice echoed eerily down the deserted corridors. Choosing a direction at random, Merak set off to look for his Princess.

The black asteroid hung midway between Atrios and Zeos, a huge chunk of jagged rock with pinnacles and crags that gave it a strange resemblance to some fantastic castle in space.

Deep inside the asteroid, Princess Astra was chained to the wall of a dungeon cell, carved from the solid rock. Her clothes were tattered, her face grimy and tear stained and she was both terrified and exhausted.

Looming over her was the sinister figure of the Shadow, his hooded servants at his heels.

'Tell me,' he hissed. 'Where is the sixth segment? You must know. You are a daughter of the Royal House of Atrios.'

'I tell you I've never heard of any sixth segment!'

'And I tell you, Princess, that the secret has been passed down through generation after generation of the Royal House. Since you are the only surviving member of that line, then you must know. You will tell me if I have to tear the secret from the living fibre of your very being. Do you understand?'

'Yes ...' sobbed Astra. 'If I knew I'd tell you—but I don't!'

The Shadow's voice was implacable. 'You do know, and you will tell me. Since you care so little for your own life, let us see how much you care for another.'

The Shadow waved a hand, and a vision screen appeared magically on the opposite wall. On it Merak could be seen, wandering disconsolately through the endless orange corridors of Zeos. 'Astra!' he called, 'Astra where are you?'

'Merak, I'm here,' shouted Astra.

The Shadow lauged evilly. 'You little fool! You think you are still on Zeos? You are not within a million miles of your precious Merak.' He waved his hand again, and the screen disappeared.

Astra slumped in her chains. 'Not on Zeos? Then where am I? What is this place?'

The Shadow leaned over her, eyes gleaming in the skull-like face. 'This Princess, is *my* domain—the Planet of Evil. Now, if you value your life, and Merak's, tell me where to find the sixth segment.'

'I can't,' sobbed Astra. *'I can't!'*

The Shadow straightened up. Astra was terrified to the point of total hysteria, too frightened to conceal anything. She was telling the truth.

Brooding in his command chair, the Marshal realised that a familiar presence was lacking. 'Where's Shapp?'

A technician hurried forward. 'We've had another intruder report from K block, Marshal. Major Shapp went to investigate.'

'At a time like this? Just as I am planning to strike a fatal blow at Zeos? I want every available ship ...'

'There is only one ship left operational, sir. Your escape——' Hurriedly he corrected himself. 'Your command vessel sir.'

'Then make it ready. And arm the missiles with atomic war-heads.'

Romana watched K9 trying to pick the transmat lock

for the second time. 'Hurry, K9!'

'The lock appears to be jammed, Mistress.'

'Then blast it out!'

'There is risk of damaging the transmat mechanism.'

'Blast it!'

K9 fired and a smoking hole appeared in place of the lock. The door sprang open. 'Right, in you go K9.'

K9 trundled into the cubicle and Romana followed. There was a flash of light as the transmat beam cut in, and they disappeared.

A few minutes later, Shapp hurried into the room hot on their trail. He went up to the open door, stepped cautiously into the cubicle—and disappeared in a flash of light.

Romana stood looking up and down the endless orange corridors of Zeos. 'We'd better split up, K9. You go and look for the Doctor, I'll try and find Merak and get the Tracer back.'

'Affirmative, Mistress.'

They went their separate ways.

Not long after they had disappeared, Shapp materialised and stumbled dazedly out into the corridor. Not sure what had happened to him, he lifted his wrist-communicator. 'Shapp to control, Shapp to control.' There was no reply—not surprisingly since control was now several million miles away.

Puzzled, Shapp stared at the silent communicator. Then he heard footsteps coming towards him. Drawing his blaster, he ducked behind a pillar.

The Doctor appeared round the corner and stood

looking thoughtfully at the transmat cubicle. 'Now, I wonder ...'

Shapp stepped up behind him, and jammed a blaster into his back. 'Turn round slowly, Doctor, and put your hands in the air.'

The Doctor obeyed. 'Paranoid as ever, Shapp. It's all right, I'm not armed.'

Shapp patted the Doctor's pockets swiftly, and stepped back. 'What happened to me? How did I get here?'

The Doctor nodded towards the cubicle. 'Through the transmat, I imagine.'

'Which sector of Atrios is this, I don't recognise it.'

'Hardly surprising, Shapp. We're on Zeos. You came through a matter transmitter.'

Nonsense,' said Shapp stoutly. 'How can we be on Zeos? This must be some prohibited part of Atrios somewhere I've never seen.'

The Doctor sighed, 'Face it, Shapp, old chap, this is Zeos!'

Still wandering the corridors, Merak was delighted to pick up a faint signal on the Tracer. He followed it to its source—a small gold bracelet lying in a dusty corner. 'Astra!' he whispered and picked it up.

He heard footsteps and ducked behind a pillar, raising the Tracer like a club.

Someone came round the corner. Merak stepped out and raised the Tracer, then checked himself as he realised the someone was Romana.

She whirled round, and grappled with him, twist-

64

ing one arm behind him so that he couldn't move. Holding him with one hand she snatched the Tracer from his grasp. 'Now listen to me Merak, I want to find Astra as much as you do. If I let you go, will you promise not to give me any more trouble?'

Merak nodded, and Romana released him.

Merak rubbed his arm. 'I'm sorry Romana. I've just got to find Astra. I know she's here now. Look!' He held up the bracelet. 'This is hers, I gave it to her. I found it over there.'

Romana held the bracelet to the Tracer. There was a faint electronic buzz.

'You see,' said Merak triumphantly.

Romana nodded thoughtfully. No doubt about it, there was some close connection between the sixth segment and the missing Princess Astra. But what?

'Come on, Merak, we'd better go on looking for her.'

The Doctor was continuing his exploration, followed reluctantly by the sceptical Shapp, who was still arguing.

'If this is Zeos, Doctor, where are the Zeons?'

'Perhaps they don't use this area.'

'Why not? The air's good, there's no radiation.' Shapp tapped the rad-scanner in his lapel. 'But the place looks as if no one's been here for years.'

The Doctor stopped suddenly and slapped his pockets. He was pretty sure that Romana and K9 would have followed him to Zeos. He produced the silver whistle, set it to his lips and blew hard. 'Should have thought of that before,' he muttered. 'Tell me,

Shapp, have you ever seen a Zeon?'

'Not since I was a child. We traded with them, before the war.'

'They weren't gaunt emaciated creatures in black robes by any chance, like the chaps who brought me here?'

'No of course not. They were people, just like us. Maybe they've mutated because of the radiation.'

'Hardly likely is it—with none of your attacks getting through!

Shapp gave him a baffled look. 'They must have been Zeons. What else could they be?'

Before the Doctor could answer, K9 trundled around the corner.

The Doctor bent down and patted him delightedly. 'What have you been up to then, eh?'

'I have been communicating with the Commander of Zeos, Master.'

'Have you now? I think you'd better take us to meet him!'

'This way, Master.'

'Hang on, let's find Romana and Merak first. We can all go and see the Commander together.'

'This way, Master!'

K9 set off at a brisk pace and the Doctor hurried after him. 'You seem in very good fettle, K9!'

'Query: fettle?'

'Form. Condition. Tone.'

'Affirmative. It is stimulating to communicate with something other than limited organic intelligences.'

'Other?'

'Affirmative, Master. I have been communicating with my own kind—the Commander of Zeos.'

The Marshal was watching the transmission of a speech he had recorded just a few minutes earlier. Now it was being broadcast to the people of Atrios —those few of them who had survived.

'The time of retribution has arrived! I myself am about to lead the final assault on Zeos itself, to deliver such a crushing blow that the spectre of Zeon aggression shall never rise again. Victory and death, my people. Victory for us, and death to our foes!'

There was a surge of martial music and the Marshal's image faded from the screen, to be replaced by the eagle crest of Atrios.

Sitting in his command chair the Marshal gave a nod of satisfaction. He always enjoyed watching his own speeches.

A technician approached and saluted. 'Your command ship is ready, Marshal. The missiles are loaded and the pilot briefed.'

The Marshal rose and strode eagerly from the War Room.

Minutes later, his command ship blasted off and set course for Zeos—armed with enough atomic missiles to devastate the planet.

It didn't take long for K9 to track down Romana and Merak. After hurried greetings and explanations, they all set off to see K9's mysterious Commander.

As they followed K9 along the corridors, Romana showed the Doctor the gold bracelet. 'The thing is, Doctor, it only gives off the faintest of signals on the Tracer. Since it's obviously not the sixth segment, what is it?'

'I'd say it was something that had recently been in contact with the segment—wouldn't you?'

'Has K9 mentioned Astra?' asked Merak. 'Is she with this Zeon Commander?'

'We'll soon know,' said the Doctor reassuringly.

K9 had come to a halt outside a huge arched door. 'Remain here, please, in silence.'

K9 gave out a complicated musical sounding sequence of electronic bleeps.

'What's he doing?' whispered Romana.

'I don't know,' said the Doctor simply. 'I've never seen him do it before.'

'Silence, please,' said K9 reprovingly. 'Communication in progress.'

Another sequence of musical bleeps, and suddenly the door slid open.

'Remain here, please.' K9 glided through.

Romana looked at the Doctor. 'Maybe it was an identification ritual—like the dance of the bees?'

K9 reappeared in the doorway, rather like an electronic butler. 'The Commander will see you now.'

They followed him through the arch, and found themselves in a long beautifully proportioned room, with soft lights bathing its glowing orange walls. The air was warm and still, and only a faint, distant hum broke the heavy silence.

At the far end of the hall was a raised dais. On the dais stood a great silver pyramid, a complex automated console behind it. There was a digital countdown clock in the centre of the console.

K9 glided to the foot of the pyramid and gave out another sequence of musical bleeps.

The pyramid glowed faintly, and gave out more

68

bleeps in reply. Clearly a conversation was taking place.

The Doctor led the others forward. 'There's your enemy, Shapp. I imagine it runs everything, attack, defence, production, surveillance. A war computer. The ideal leader, no glory, no speeches, no medals ... The whole planet is automated. There are no Zeons on this part of Zeos.'

'Where are they then?'

'On the other side of the planet, I imagine, some-where in hiding. But before they went, they set this up. And it's been fighting a robot war for them ever since.' The Doctor looked up at the pyramid. 'A passionless lump of mineral and electronic circuitry, highly efficient. It's given Atrios a battering, killed millions probably, without a flicker of emotion. Just doing its job—and it's absolutely invincible.'

Shapp drew his blaster. 'We'll see about that!'

As he raised the weapon a ray shot out from a row of muzzles set into the wall behind the pyramid. Shapp yelped, and the blaster fell from his numbed fingers.

'It's got an automatic defence system!'

Merak said, 'Doctor, please what about Astra?'

The Doctor nodded, 'K9, could you ask your friend here if the name of Princess Astra rings a bell.'

K9 gave off a sequence of bleeps, and the computer replied in kind.

K9 said, 'All information regarding Princess Astra is inaccessible.'

There were more bleeps from the computer.

K9 said, 'Mentalis also informs me that the war is now over. The next step is obliteration.'

69

'Obliteration?' said the Doctor sharply. 'For whom?'

There was a single bleep from the computer.

K9 translated. 'For everything.'

The Marshal's ship was speeding towards Zeos. The pilot looked up from the controls. 'Target located, sir.'

In the co-pilot's seat, the Marshal leaned forward eagerly. 'Excellent! Prepare to attack!'

9

The Armageddon Factor

Romana and Merak were standing a little apart, looking on anxiously as the Doctor engaged in a long conversation with Mentalis, using K9 as his interpreter.

After a final flurry of bleeps, the Doctor turned away. 'It's no use. Mentalis won't tell us anything about Astra and refuses all access to its memory banks. It did tell me something else, though, something rather disturbing.'

'What's that?' asked Romana apprehensively.

'Mentalis has been programmed that the war is over. Which means it can't attack. But according to Shapp, the Marshal will soon be on his way here with the intention of blowing Zeos to smithereens.'

Romana frowned. 'Surely Mentalis will react.'

The Doctor nodded. 'Oh yes, Mentalis is convinced its invincible. It isn't programmed to accept defeat.'

'So what will it do?'

'Fire a salvo of automated missiles that will totally obliterate Atrios, and then self-destruct. The term it used was obliteration. So if the Marshal attacks, first Atrios will be destroyed and then a rather big bang will blow up the whole of Zeos. The war will end in a draw. It's the way these military minds work, you see. Destruction rather than defeat. You could call it the Armageddon Factor.' He looked round the circle of worried faces and went on, 'Has it ever occurred to you Shapp, that you and the Marshal *and* Mentalis here might all be in a kind of interplanetary arena, playing out this game for the benefit of some alien, evil spectator?'

'You mean there's a kind of third force involved, Doctor?' asked Romana.

'Oh yes, and I think I've met him. Calls himself the Shadow ...'

Flanked by mute, hooded guards, the Shadow appeared in the doorway of Princess Astra's cell.

He moved towards her, and she screamed and strained away, tugging vainly against her chains.

The Shadow moved closer, closer, ... He stretched out his skeletal hand to her throat ... Princess Astra arched her back and screamed—then went suddenly still and silent.

When the Shadow stepped back, there was a small black cylinder at her throat.

The Shadow spoke. 'Princess Astra, do you hear me?'

'I hear you Master.'

'Good. There are duties you must perform. You will help me in my quest, do you understand?'

'Yes, Master.'

'You are to meet your lover soon, Princess. Smile!'

Astra smiled. It was like a grimace on the face of a corpse.

The Doctor had made his plans and was outlining

them to his companions. 'I've got to work out a way to neutralise Mentalis—and there mustn't be any attack from the Marshal while I'm doing it. Merak, you and Shapp have got to go back to Atrios via the transmat. Tell the Marshal the war is over; tell him he's won. Tell him anything, but don't let him attack Zeos!'

'Suppose he won't listen?' asked Shapp.

'He's got to. If the Marshal attacks, Mentalis will trigger the Armageddon sequence. Bang! Both planets will end up as bits of dust floating around the cosmos—including the Marshal. Tell him that!' He looked impatiently at them. 'Well, go on, what are you waiting for?'

'What about Astra?' said Merak.

Romana put a hand on his arm. 'If she's here we'll find her. You can do more good on Atrios, helping Shapp to convince the Marshal.'

Merak nodded, and went out after Shapp. He was hurrying to catch up when he heard a voice. 'Merak!'

Merak paused listening.

The voice came again. 'Merak . . . Merak . . .' It was Astra.

Shapp paused at the junction that led to the transmat cubicle. 'What are you doing, Merak? Come on!' He hurried to the door of the cubicle and paused, looking back the way he had come. 'Come on Merak. Hurry, man!'

Merak was nowhere to be seen. Shapp heard a slither of movement behind him and swung round.

At the other end of the corridor a black-hooded,

skull-faced figure was aiming a blaster at him.

As the figure fired, Shapp sprang aside, and the energy-bolt seared across his shoulder.

Shapp fired one wild shot in return, and staggered into the transmat cubicle.

The white light flared up, and he disappeared.

Merak meanwhile was following Astra's ghostly voice. 'It's me Astra,' he called. 'It's me, Merak!'

'Merak,' called the ghostly voice. 'Come to me, Merak.'

Merak found himself in a long dark corridor that seemed to stretch ahead for ever. In the distance he saw Astra, stretching out her arms to him. 'Merak.'

He ran towards her. He came closer, closer, stretched out his arms to embrace her.

His arms passed through her ghostly body, the ground disappeared beneath his feet.

The empty corridor was filled with the mocking laughter of the Shadow.

The Doctor removed a panel from the side of the gleaming pyramid, glancing uneasily at the automated blasters. 'You're sure this is all right, K9? Your friend isn't feeling threatened at all?'

'Negative, Master. Proceed.'

The Doctor began dis-connecting circuits with his sonic screwdriver. Romana watched him work. 'Doctor, do you think the Shadow built this computer?'

'Not personally, perhaps. But I think he had a hand in it.'

'And it's the Shadow who's got the Princess?'

'More than likely. The question is, where?'

Romana held a hand before the Doctor's eyes. 'You said there must be something between Atrios and Zeos.'

The Doctor looked up. 'Yes, of course! Romana, you're brilliant. He must have a base, perhaps a third planet of his own.'

'So all we have to do is find it.'

The Doctor resumed work. 'When we've dealt with this. If we can deal with it ...'

The Doctor removed a circuit from the inside of the pyramid; there was a chorus of alarmed bleeps.

'Doctor, what have you done?'

The Doctor scratched his head. 'I'm not sure. What have I done, K9?'

'You have triggered the primary alert function. The computer will now self-destruct, if required to resist attack.'

The Doctor went on working. 'Let's hope Shapp gets to the Marshal in time. We're rather vulnerable until this is done.'

There were more bleeps from the computer, these too with a definite note of alarm about them.

'Hostile craft approaching,' announced K9.

An array of red lights began flashing on the console behind the pyramid.

'That'll be the Marshal,' said the Doctor grimly. 'Shapp must have been too late.'

There was a final crescendo of agitated bleeps. 'Mentalis has now entered self-destruct sequence,' announced K9.

A loud ticking came from the digital clock. It began counting down from 1000. 999 ... 998 ... 997.

The Doctor began working at frantic speed. 'It'll blow itself up and us with it, if it's attacked. Unless I can ...'

'Look out, Doctor!' shrieked Romana.

The Doctor flung himself backwards as the automatic blasters trained themselves on the pyramid and fired in unison. The pyramid exploded in a shower of sparks.

The Doctor opened his eyes, relieved to find himself still alive. 'That was close!'

Romana helped him to pick himself up. 'How did they all manage to miss you?'

'They weren't aiming at me, they were aiming at that.' The Doctor nodded towards the shattered pyramid. 'Like the scorpion stinging itself to death. As soon as it sensed I was trying to stop the Armageddon sequence it destroyed its own control centre. It's mindless now.'

The steady ticking went on. 820, 819, 818 ...

'Oh well,' said the Doctor philosophically, 'If at first you don't succeed—get out fast! Come on!'

He sprinted for the door, Romana and K9 close behind him.

They hurried along the endless deserted corridors until they reached the room in which the Doctor had been interrogated by the Shadow. To the Doctor's delight, the TARDIS was still there, and they dashed inside.

Once in the control room, the Doctor went over to a hidden wall safe. Opening it with his palm print, he took out a large chunk of gleaming crystal—there was an irregularly shaped gap in the crystal's side. The Doctor held it up. There! Look at that. What do you see?'

Romana looked. 'Five of the six pieces put together. How does that help?'

'Well, perhaps five pieces out of six gives us five-sixths of the power—provided Guardian technology works that way.'

'If only we had the sixth piece ...'

'Or *a* sixth piece,' said the Doctor suddenly. 'We can see the shape of the missing piece—and if we know that, we can make one!'

Clutching the crystal, the Doctor hurried off to the TARDIS workshop.

In the Marshal's command ship the pilot said, 'Zeos ahead, sir.'

The Marshal stared hungrily at the mist-covered globe below. 'At last! I shall crush it like a rotten egg. Prepare to fire ...'

The pilot touched a control, and the ship vibrated with a smooth hum of machinery as the rocket racks slid into firing position. 'Missiles armed and targetted, sir. We'll be in range shortly.'

'Go in close,' ordered the Marshal. 'As close as you possibly can.'

A voice crackled from the control panel. 'Atrian control to Marshal. This is Major Shapp. Imperative you abort mission. The war is over. Abort your mission!'

'Turn that thing off,' growled the Marshal. 'Damn bureaucrats, trying to steal my thunder. *I'll* put an end to this war. Prepare for rocket strike.'

The pilot's hand reached for the red firing button.

'Wait for the order,' growled the Marshal. 'We're not quite close enough ...'

*

The Doctor hurried back into the TARDIS control room. In one hand he held the incomplete Key to Time, in the other an oddly shaped chunk of crystal. It was duller than the crystals comprising the Key, with a yellowish tinge to it. 'Well, here's the spare part.'

Romana looked dubiously at it. 'What did you use?'

'Chronodyne.'

'Is it compatible?'

'It's as compatible as anything we've got.'

'Compatability ratio seventy-four per cent,' droned K9. 'Component therefore unstable, and liable to deteriorate.'

The Doctor fitted the imitation sixth segment into place. 'In theory, this should give us powers of balance. We should be able to create a neutral, timeless zone over the entire area—at least for a time ... Give me the Tracer, Romana, I need it to seal the chronodyne in place.' He fitted the Tracer into a kind of socket in the base of the crystal.

The Marshal gazed through the viewing port at the curve of Zeos close below.

'Fire!' he yelled.

The pilot's finger reached for the button ...

'Fire!' yelled the Marshal.

The pilot's finger reached for the button ...

And reached for the button ...

In the computer room, the countdown clock was reading 10, 9, 8 ... 10, 9, 8 ... 10, 9, 8 ...

Over and over again.

Romana looked up from the TARDIS console. 'I've got them, Doctor!'

The Doctor hurried over.

On the scanner he saw the Marshal's ship streaking towards Zeos ... and streaking towards Zeos ... and streaking towards Zeos ... Over and over again. 'We did it,' said the Doctor exultantly. 'Ninety-nine per cent success.'

'Ninety-nine point five four,' corrected K9.

'Even better. We've got them in a time loop! We're gods for an hour, you might say ...'

'Negative,' interrupted K9. 'Deterioration of chronodyne crystal is in direct ratio to area affected. Probable duration three point two five minutes.'

The Doctor was horrified. 'Three and a quarter minutes? We've got to concentrate the effect.' He looked at Romana and K9. 'I suppose if one had god-like powers one just has to use them in a god-like way.' He held up the Key and looked hard at it. 'I command ...' He cleared his throat. 'Better get this right, hadn't I ... I command that the spatio temporal loop be confined to the immediate vicinity of the Marshal's vessel ...'

'And the computer room,' urged Romana.

'And the computer room,' added the Doctor hurriedly. He beamed. 'There! I thought that went rather well, didn't you?'

'All power corrupts,' said Romana reprovingly.

'Oh, come on, it's only a three second time loop. How's the chronodyne crystal, K9, still deteriorating?'

'Affirmative. Chronodyne deteriorating but at a much slower rate.'

'I hoped you'd say that.' The Doctor rummaged in a locker, produced a carved oak pedestal, and put the Key to Time on top of it. 'Still, I think we'd better get moving. Nothing lasts forever, not even my time loops!'

Princess Astra stood in the middle of a circle of darkness, the Shadow close beside her. She was in a huge circular room, furnished only with a raised dais on which stood a throne. It was the lair of the Shadow.

'The Doctor has been forced to use the Key,' hissed the Shadow. 'Therefore it is no longer safe in limbo. You will lure the Doctor here and help me to gain access to the TARDIS. Do you understand.'

'I understand, Master,' said Astra dully. A filmy white scarf concealed the control cylinder on her throat.

'Come. My servants will go with you in the transmat.' Beckoning the hooded mutes, the Shadow led Astra away.

10

The Planet of Evil

Merak awoke to find himself lying at the bottom of a shallow steel shaft. One leg was twisted awkwardly under him, and it throbbed painfully when he tried to move.

A familiar voice called, 'Merak? Merak, are you all right?' He looked up. Princess Astra was standing at the edge of the pit looking down at him.

'Are you badly hurt?' she called.

Merak clambered painfully to his feet. 'I think my leg's twisted. What happened?'

'I called out to you, and you ran towards me and fell. I tried to save you, but you stumbled past me in the darkness.'

'I thought you were a ghost,' said Merak dazedly. He looked around him. The shaft wasn't all that deep, in fact by stretching up he could just reach the edge with his fingers. Its walls were covered with dials and heavy cables; Merak guessed he'd stumbled into some kind of inspection pit.

'Here, let me help you,' called Astra. She leaned over the edge of the pit and caught his hand. Merak gripped the edge of the pit with his other hand and with Astra's help, managed to heave himself over the edge of the shaft. 'We must find the Doctor ...'

'Here—put your arm around my neck,' said Astra,

and helped him to hobble along the corridor.

Two black-hooded figures trailed them through the darkness.

The Doctor had heaved out most of the innards of the pyramid by now, and was sorting, somewhat despairingly through a tangled mass of wires and circuitry.

'Doesn't look very hopeful, does it?' said Romana.

'No. Whoever built this computer had a very twisted mind! There must be a fail-safe cut-out somewhere—but I just can't find it!' He went back to work.

K9 was guarding the door of the room which held the TARDIS. He alerted at the sound of approaching footsteps. 'Who goes there? Identify yourself.'

Merak came round the corner, helped along by Astra. 'It's all right, K9, it's me, Merak.'

'Identify second humanoid.'

'This is the Princess Astra. The Doctor wants her to help him.'

Merak hobbled forward. K9 said sharply, 'Wait! Hostile presence detected.'

'Where?'

'Hostiles approaching. Take cover.'

Astra and Merak ducked into the room, just as two black-hooded mutes appeared along down the corridor, blasters in hand.

K9 advanced firing, and the two mutes turned and fled. Still blazing away, K9 glided off in pursuit.

Princess Astra was staring at the TARDIS, which seemed to hold some strange fascination for her. 'What is inside?' she whispered. 'I must see inside.'

'I'm sorry, only the Doctor and Romana can get in.'

Astra looked strangely at him and said, 'Yes, of course. K9 has driven off the attackers. Now we must go and find your friends.'

With K9 close behind them the mutes scuttled back to the transmat cubicle, hurried inside and disappeared in a blaze of light.

'Satisfactory,' said K9, giving himself a mental pat on the back. 'Hostiles have been repulsed.'

There was another flash, and a plain black box materialised in the cubicle. It was giving off a regular series of bleeps in a repeating pattern.

K9 glided forward curiously. 'Distress call has been received. Please identify source of transmission.'

The box continued to bleep.

K9 glided into the cubicle.

There was a flash of light, and K9 and the box dematerialised.

The Doctor looked up as Merak hobbled into the computer room, half-supported by Princess Astra.

'Doctor, I've found her! This is the Princess Astra.'

The Doctor rose and bowed. 'I'm very pleased to meet you, Your Highness. This is my friend Romana.' He turned back to Merak. 'Did you rescue her?'

Ruefully, Merak shook his head. 'She escaped, all by herself, then she rescued me!' He told the Doctor what had happened.

The Doctor looked admiringly at Astra. 'Escaped, eh?' How did you manage that?'

'I managed to slip away from my guards, and I hid in a kind of cubicle. There was a flash of light, and I found myself here. The guards followed me, but your—K9 chased them away.'

'Good, good,' said the Doctor absently. He looked at his unfinished task. 'Tell you what, Your Highness, why don't you take Merak back to Atrios, through the transmat.'

'I'd feel safer with you, Doctor.'

'That's very kind of you, but we've got a very tricky job to finish. The best thing you can do is go home and let your people know you're safe.'

Merak took Astra's arm. 'The Doctor's right, Astra. Come along. How do I set the controls for Atrios?'

The Doctor gave him brief instructions, and they hurried away.

K9 emerged from the transmat cubicle and found himself in a gloomy tunnel of rock. 'This is not Atrios. Nor is it Zeos. What is this place?'

The only answer was a mocking echo. 'This place ... this place ... this place ...'

Then a husky, sinister voice whispered, 'Welcome to my domain. I am the Shadow!'

Before K9 could move, a black robed figure swooped down on him, and clamped a metal cylinder beneath his chin.

The Doctor rose to his feet. 'It's no good Romana. We'll just have to try something else.'

'Such as?'

'Finding the real sixth segment. If we can do that, all our troubles will be over. I can put this computer in a permanent time loop if necessary.' He led the way from the room.

'Where are we going, Doctor?'

'To the third planet, Romana. The lair of the Shadow!'

Merak pointed. 'There it is, Astra. The transmat cubicle.'

Suddenly Astra thrust him away from her. Merak's leg buckled beneath him, and he fell.

'Astra what are you doing? Help me up?'

Astra's mouth twisted in a sneer. 'I have more important things to do.'

The transmat flared with light and two armed mutes appeared. Astra beckoned them towards her.

'You're not Astra,' gasped Merak. 'Who are you?'

'You are a fool,' said Astra coldly. She led the two mutes away. Gritting his teeth against the pain, Merak crawled slowly towards the transmat.

When the Doctor and Romana reached the TARDIS, K9 was nowhere to be seen. 'Perhaps he's still chasing those guards,' suggested Romana.

The Doctor held up his hand. 'Listen!'

They heard blaster fire, a sudden scream, frantic footsteps hurrying towards them.

Princess Astra burst into the room. 'Doctor, help me. They're after me!'

'Quick, into the TARDIS,' said Romana. She took Astra's hand and pulled her to the door.

The Doctor followed them, patting his pockets. 'Key, key, key, now where did I—Ah, here we are!'

He opened the door and they hurried inside.

The Doctor closed the door behind them, and Astra stood looking around her in astonishment.

The Doctor hurried over to the scanner, where the Marshal's command ship was still going through its repeated sequence.

Romana looked over his shoulder. 'Looks as if the loop's stretched to about five seconds.'

The Doctor nodded. 'That gives us about an hour of real time.' He turned to Astra. 'What happened to Merak?'

'I got him to the transmat cubicle but the guards turned up so I led them away from him. He ought to be safe by now.'

Romana said, 'I'll try to get a fix on the third planet.'

Astra was staring raptly at the Key to Time. 'What is it?'

'That, my dear, is the Key to Time, or five sixths of it.' The Doctor looked curiously at her. 'Are you sure you're all right, Princess?'

'Perfectly, Doctor.'

'Does the Key trigger any hidden memory?'

'No. It means nothing to me.'

The Doctor rubbed his chin. 'Pity! If it did, you might be able to tell us where the real sixth segment could be found. We're looking for the final clue. Think Astra, think!'

Astra walked slowly forward to the Key and reached

out her hand.

'I shouldn't touch it,' said the Doctor sharply. 'It's hot!'

The chronodyne crystal replacing the sixth segment was beginning to overheat, sizzling faintly and giving off wisps of smoke.

Romana said suddenly, 'Got it Doctor! A kind of giant asteroid, midway between the two planets. It's heavily shielded.'

'Well done, Romana. Set the co-ordinates, and we'll be on our way.'

Princess Astra was still staring at the Key to Time.

The Shadow stood in his lair, listening to the TARDIS materialisation sound echoing through the rocky corridors of his domain. K9 was at his feet.

The Shadow looked down. 'Your friends are arriving, it seems. We must go and greet them.'

'Affirmative, Master.'

The Shadow threw back his skull-like head, and a peal of demoniacal laughter merged with the sound of the TARDIS.

'You are a fool to enter my domain, Doctor. Soon the Key to Time will be mine!'

11

Drax

The centre column of the TARDIS console stopped its rise and fall, and the Doctor drew a deep breath. 'Well, here we are. We've tracked the Shadow to his lair.'

Romana said ironically. 'That's right. We've got him exactly where he wants us!'

The Doctor nodded towards the pedestal. 'All we've got to do now is get hold of the sixth piece—without letting the Shadow get his hands on the other five!'

'How can we find the sixth segment without using the Tracer? And we can't use the Tracer because it's holding the Key together. If we take the Tracer out we lose the time loop, and if that goes, millions of people on Atrios and Zeos will die!' Romana looked at the imitation segment, now cracked and smoking. 'How much longer is that thing going to last anyway?'

The Doctor shrugged. 'We need a bit of diagonal thinking, don't we Princess?'

Astra was staring at the Key. 'What? I'm sorry, I was miles away.'

'We need your help in finding the Shadow and the Key.'

'Can't I stay here?'

'No, Astra. You've been to this place before. We need your help.'

'*I want to stay here!*'

Romana looked at her in surprise. 'Don't you want to help us save Atrios?'

'My destiny no longer lies with Atrios.'

(A husky voice sounded inside Astra's head. 'Go with them. You will bring me Romana.')

Astra looked up. 'I understand.'

Romana looked curiously at her. 'Are you all right?'

The Doctor said, 'Everything's perfect, isn't it, Astra?'

'Of course. I will come with you, Doctor. We must do everything we can to defeat the Shadow.'

'Do you know where he is?' asked Romana.

'I think I can find him.'

The Doctor opened the door, and Astra led the way out of the TARDIS. 'I'll be right with you,' said the Doctor. 'Just locking up.' He went back to the TARDIS console, and listened for a moment, adjusting the tuning on the audio circuits. A regular repetitive pattern of bleeps filled the control room. 'I thought I heard something. Pan-galactic distress signal. How very odd!'

The Doctor rummaged in a locker and took out a compass-like audio-tracer and hurried after the others.

The black asteroid was honeycombed with twisted tunnels and passageways, supported by columns of stone, lit only by a sinister green glow that seemed to come from the rock itself. Here and there caves led off from the tunnels. Some were no more than tiny cells, others were immense gloomy halls. All were dark and silent. The dank air was full of distant clanking and groaning sounds, the squeak of bats and the scurrying of tiny rat-like creatures. Here and there carved gargoyle faces leered from the solid rock. The whole place had a strange organic feel, like a rotten apple bored through by innumerable worms.

Romana and Astra hurried on. Romana glanced over her shoulder for the Doctor. He seemed to be taking a very long time.

From an alcove, K9 stood watching them, a black robed figure beside him.

'Instructions, Master?'

'Leave Romana to Astra. You will follow the Doctor.'

'Affirmative, Master.'

Audio-tracer in hand, the Doctor hurried out of the TARDIS. He studied the readings. 'Two six zero,' he muttered and thrust the device in his pocket.

He could just see Romana and Astra in the distance. 'Wait for me, you two. If we don't stick together, we'll all get lost.'

Suddenly Romana and Astra vanished.

The Doctor hurried after them, and found himself at a point where several tunnels joined.

'Doctor!' called Romana's mocking voice. Romana stood at the end of one of the passages.

'Doctor!' called the voice again, and Romana was in another passage too.

'Doctor! Doctor! Doctor!' called the voices and suddenly different versions of Romana stood *in all* the passages at once.

The mocking laughter of the Shadow filled the tunnels.

The Doctor shouted, 'You'll have to do better than that!'

Romana paused and looked behind her. 'What does he think he's doing? Surely he saw us!'

Astra was looking around her. 'I remember now, all these tunnels link up, just ahead. If we hurry on this way we'll run straight into him.'

Since the Doctor had lost Romana, he decided to concentrate on tracing the distress signal. He took the audio-tracer from his pocket and checked the reading again. 'Two seven five ...' He hurried on, and was rather surprised to meet himself going in the opposite direction.

'Excuse me,' said the Doctor politely, and stepped aside to let himself by.

Realising, he spun round. There was no one there.

The Doctor smiled grimly, and addressed the nearest gargoyle. 'I can see what you're doing ... splitting us all up. Divide and rule, eh? Rather an ancient tactic.'

The gargoyle stared blankly back at him. The Doctor laughed. 'You didn't really imagine I was taken in by Astra—did you Shadow?'

In the Shadow's lair, the Doctor's face was on a wall screen. His voice echoed cheerfully through the gloomy chamber. 'She's in your power, isn't she? Little something on the neck, eh? Pretty crude technologically.'

The Shadow snarled.

*

In his tunnel the Doctor chatted cheerily to the gargoyle head, confident that it was transmitting all his words to the Shadow. 'All this penny arcade, ghost train rubbish is pretty crude too. Romana can look after herself you know. You won't scare her with spooks.' A giant spider dropped onto the Doctor's shoulder and he flicked it casually away. 'Or me either. We're Time Lords you know, not like those poor innocents from Zeos and Atrios you've been playing games with. Time Lords, sent by the Guardian—to recover the Key to Time!'

Suddenly the Doctor saw the Shadow standing before him.

'I know who you are, Doctor. I have always known. I have been waiting for you.'

The Shadow's voice echoed through the tunnels, as though the asteroid itself was speaking. 'I too serve a Guardian, Doctor. A Guardian equal and opposite to your own. The Black Guardian. He Who Walks in Darkness.' There was a roar of mocking laughter. 'And you Doctor, are in the Valley of the Shadow!'

The Shadow vanished.

The Doctor ran forward to the spot where he had been. Suddenly the solid rock turned into a whirlpool, sucking him in ...

K9 glided from the shadow. 'The Doctor is captured —Master.'

Princess Astra paused by an arched stone doorway and beckoned. 'Come, Romana. You'll be quite safe in here!'

As Romana came into the room an enormous black-hooded mute sprang from the shadows and lifted her in his arms. Kicking and screaming, Romana was borne away.

Princess Astra smiled.

The Doctor recovered consciousness in a dungeon. It was a very old-fashioned dungeon; stone-block walls, studded iron door, high barred windows ... Clearly the Shadow had traditional tastes in such matters.

There was a strange rythmic bleeping ...

The Doctor hunted round the cell and found a plain black box tucked into one corner. He studied it thoughtfully.

He heard a sliding, grating sound. One of the stone blocks that made up the inner wall was slowly moving forward. It moved further, further, it dropped free and thudded to the ground. The Doctor jumped back, and waited to see what would happen next.

A head appeared in the gap, a round, close cropped head with a set of cheerfully villanious features. It spoke. 'Ullo, Thete, How are you, boy?'

The Doctor stared. 'What?' he said faintly.

'It is Thete, innit? Old Theta Sigma? Course it is! Remember me?'

Narrow shoulders appeared behind the head and began squeezing through the gap. Wriggling eel-like through the hole, the newcomer dropped through to the floor, and then sprang to his feet. He was a small, lithe man in shabby space-coveralls. He looked cheerily up at the Doctor. 'You remember me, Thete? Drax is the name. Class of ninety-three. We was on the technical course together. Long time ago now, Thete, must be what, four hundred and fifty years? We're a long way from Gallifrey eh?'

'Of course,' said the Doctor. 'Drax! We were at the Academy together.'

'That's right. Till they slung me out. I was all right on the practical, see, it was temporal theory done me in.' He shook his head sadly. 'Still, you done all right, getting your Doctorate and all that. Though I did hear you was in a spot of bother later. Taking and driving away a TARDIS without the owner's consent. Naughty, naughty. Got done by the High Court, didn't you? Served a stretch in exile. Earth ... wasn't it?'

The Doctor cleared his throat. 'Oh, that was all forgiven and forgotten long ago. What happened to you?'

'Well, I bought this second-hand TARDIS— bought, not nicked Thete—and went into repairs and maintenance didn't I? Do anything, go anywhere, all over the galaxy. Buy a bit, do it up, sell it again. Cybernetics, guidance systems, you name it.'

'Arms?' suggested the Doctor gently.

'Well, that too. Not on a regular basis, mind. And computers. No one to touch me on computers.'

'I was introduced to a computer called Mentalis on Zeos. Did you build that?'

'That's right. Soon as I'd finished the job I found myself here. Kidnapped by the Shadow.' Drax spotted the black box and pounced on it. 'That's where I left it. Thought someone must have pinched it.' He studied the box for a moment then switched it off. 'Not that it ever done me much good!'

'You made that thing—here?'

'Never go nowhere without me tools, do I?'

'Drax, I hope you don't mind my being personal—but where did you acquire that accent and vocabulary?'

'Brixton, wannit?' said Drax proudly. 'London, Earf.' He lowered his voice to a confidential whisper. 'Transport broke down see, hyperbolics as usual. Well, I was temporarily out of funds, and I was investigating certain possibilities with regard to spare-part replacements when—well, I got done, didn't I —just like you. Ten years for knocking off top secret equipment. Well, I had to learn the language to survive, See? Why, is there anyfing wrong with the way I talk?'

'No, no,' said the Doctor hastily. 'It's very colourful, very demotic.'

'Thanks, Thete.'

'Doctor,' said the Doctor firmly. Theta Sigma wasn't his name anyway it was a kind of Time Lord coding. The Doctor didn't think he could bear being addressed as 'Thete' for the rest of their association.

'Oh, suit yourself then—Doctor,' said Drax huffily. 'We ain't all got degrees.'

'It's just that I'm used to it,' said the Doctor cajolingly. 'No offence meant, Drax, old friend.'

'And none taken—Doctor,' said the little man heartily.

The Doctor nodded at the gap in the wall. 'Might there be a way out through there?'

Drax shook his head sadly. 'No, not yet anyway. I got passages and tunnels all over the place, but I can't seem to find the transmat shaft. Trouble is, my

TARDIS is back on Zeos.'

'Where *does* it lead, then?'

'Have a look.' invited Drax.

The Doctor squeezed through the gap and found himself in a dungeon exactly like the one he'd left—except for the addition of a cluttered stone workbench and a set of tools.

A number of complex looking components were scattered on the bench, and the Doctor studied them thoughtfully. 'Aren't those stabiliser components? I thought your TARDIS was on Zeos.'

'Took the stabiliser out, didn't I? Needs a bit of work.'

The Doctor looked hard at him. 'How long have you been here, Drax?'

'Oh, must be a year or so ...'

'And you've had a dimensional stabiliser virtually intact all that time, and you haven't escaped.'

'Told you, it needs work.'

The Doctor laughed. 'Oh come on Drax. You could have had that fixed and skipped out of here years ago—*if you'd wanted to!*' He peered suspiciously at Drax's neck.

'Think I'm in with the Shadow, is that it?' asked Drax offendedly. 'Would I do such a thing?'

Yes, you would! Now I suppose you'll suggest you and I make a run for it—in my TARDIS?'

'Ooh, what a good idea,' said Drax, with unconvincing enthusiasm.

'Isn't it?' said the Doctor sardonically. 'You and I inside the TARDIS! What then, eh? Lead pipe. Sock full of wet sand? And you'd be away with the Key to Time, am I right?'

Drax nodded shamefacedly. 'Shadow threatened me with the chop, didn't he? Said I was the only one who could get hold of it.'

'And suppose you had? You think he'd let you go? You'd be for the chop for sure then.'

'Yeah, suppose you're right.'

'So why don't you help me then? *Really* help me, I mean. Together we'd stand a chance.' The Doctor put his arm round the little man's shoulders. 'After all, we are both Time Lords. Class of ninety-three and all that! I mean, if we don't stick together, who will?'

The Doctor beamed down at Drax and Drax nodded, and smiled uncertainly back.

He had the strangest feeling he'd been conned ...

12

The Bargain

Clamped into the diamond shaped cage, Romana was being interrogated by the Shadow. Every hesitation, every evasion was punished with a burst of agonising pain.

At last the questions ceased, and the Shadow turned angrily away. 'She has told me all she knows, and it is still not enough. Still the cursed Doctor stands between me and the Key!' He turned back to Romana. 'We shall see how much the Doctor values your life.'

Romana was slumped against the bars, weak but still defiant. 'He'll never give you the Key. I'm not afraid to die.'

The Shadow ignored her. 'K9, go to the Doctor. You know what to tell him.'

'Affirmative, Master.'

K9 glided away.

Drax was busy at his bench, repairing and re-assembling his stabiliser. 'You really reckon this will work, Doctor? A stabiliser-gun?'

'I don't see why not?' The Doctor watched him work for a moment. 'Try synaptic adhesion.'

'No, no. It's the chronostat, always is. I done thousands of these, Doctor. Thousands!'

'I tell you its got to be synaptic adhesion.'

Drax glared at him and put down his tools.

Hastily the Doctor said, 'I'll leave you to it then, shall I?'

'Why don't you do that?'

The Doctor looked through a gap in the other wall. 'Where does this lead, then?'

'Upper level. Look out for the mutes.'

The Doctor clambered through the gap and found himself in a long narrow tunnel. He wriggled forward on knees and elbows and after a time he saw a patch of dim light at the end. Suddenly he heard a familiar voice. 'I have you on scan, Doctor. Continue this way.'

'That was K9,' thought the Doctor in astonishment. 'He's never called me Doctor before!'

He wriggled on until he reached an iron grille. He moved it aside, and saw it was set at ground level in one of the tunnels.

Popping his head out, the Doctor found himself nose to nose with K9. 'Doctor!'

'Yes, old friend?' said the Doctor sadly. From this low level it was easy to see the black cylinder at K9's throat.

'I have a message for you.'

'Can't hear you old chap, come closer.'

K9 moved nearer, and the Doctor made a grab at the cylinder. K9 realised his intention, and re-treated rapidly. 'Such actions warrant immediate execution.'

'Oh, K9,' said the Doctor sadly.

'Here is your message. My Master has Romana. He offers you her life in exchange for the Key to

Time.' K9 paused. 'End of message. Your reply please. Waiting.'

'Tell him I'll think about it,' said the Doctor, and began climbing out of his tunnel.

He made a great business of climbing to his feet and dusting himself down. 'Right you are, K9 let's go!'

As K9 turned to lead the way, the Doctor suddenly sprang clear over him, swung him round, and shoved him through the gap. 'Sorry, K9!'

He heard K9 rattling down the steep tunnel. There was a moment's silence, then a terrible metallic crash. The Doctor winced, and called, 'You all right down there, Drax?'

After a moment an astonished voice floated up. 'Yeah, you? What's this heap of junk you've shoved down on me?'

'My computer. Listen, Drax, just get the control device from under his chin, will you?'

There was a pause then Drax's voice came again. 'Right, got it, Doctor. Now what?'

'Carry on with our little project. I'll be back soon —I hope!'

In the workshop Drax looked down at K9, who was still laying upside down on a heap of scrap, squawking angrily. 'Attention. Essential I am restored to vertical position.'

'I'm busy.'

The blaster projected from beneath K9's nose. 'Restore me to vertical position.'

'All right, all right,' said Drax hurriedly. He lifted

K9 off the scrap heap and set him down upright. 'That better?'

'Affirmative.' K9 began darting to and fro. 'Drive circuits re-stabilising.'

Drax looked on in astonishment. 'It's a dog! Who's a little tin doggie then?'

K9 ignored him.

Drax went on with his task, re-assembling the stabiliser into a vaguely gun-shaped device. He peered thoughtfully at it. 'I don't get it. It's always the chronostat.'

K9 scanned the device. 'The fault is a question of synoptic adhesion.'

Drax groaned. 'Now don't you start!'

The Doctor was moving cautiously along the tunnels when a particularly large mute appeared from the darkness before him. One enormous hand held a blaster, the other beckoned the Doctor onwards.

Resignedly the Doctor obeyed. He knew there was no real escape from the Shadow, not on the Planet of Evil. The whole place was no more than an expression of the Shadow's will.

The mute ushered the Doctor into the great cave that served as the Shadow's lair. The diamond-shaped cage stood in the centre. Romana still inside it.

Princess Astra stood near the cage, her face a blank, and the Shadow sat on his black throne. 'You will give me the Key to Time, Doctor. Or would you prefer to see your companion suffer?'

The Shadow waved his hand. Sparks crackled round the cage and Romana twisted in agony.

'Stop!' shouted the Doctor. 'I refuse to negotiate under threat.'

The sparks stopped, and Romana slumped against the bars. 'Don't give it to him, Doctor. It doesn't matter what happens to me.'

'Oh, yes it does, Romana,' said the Doctor softly. He looked at the Shadow. 'I take it you have the sixth segment here?'

'It is here, Doctor.'

'I'd like to see it, if that's possible.'

'You have already seen it Doctor,' said the Shadow mockingly.

'Oh!' Wearily the Doctor rubbed his forehead. 'Tell me, when I give you the first five segments, when you have all six—what will you do? I mean, you realise I've rigged something up to prevent the destruction of Zeos and Atrios?'

'Your puny time loop, Doctor?' sneered the Shadow.

'It may be puny, but it works. If you upset it, millions will die.'

'That has always been our intention, Doctor. This pathetic little war has been but a rehearsal for our grand design.'

'*Our* design?'

'I have my Guardian, Doctor,' said the Shadow proudly, 'just as you have yours. You and I are on the same quest. But whereas you have been scavenging through space and time. I located the sixth segment here, and waited for you to bring me the other five.' The Shadow laughed. 'Once we have the Key to Time, Doctor, we shall set not just two planets but the two halves of the cosmos at war. The sound of destruction will be music in our ears. Unlike others, we do not seek power. We glory in destruction! Chaos shall rule the cosmos once more.' The Shadow paused, gasping for breath. 'Now fetch me the Key, Doctor!'

'Very well. But not until you let Romana out of that cage.'

With a sneer the Shadow waved his hand, and the cage door sprang open. 'Well Doctor?'

The Doctor bowed his head, and the giant mute marched him away.

Drax straightened up, rubbing his back. 'You were right, little tin doggie. Synoptic adhesion it was!' He switched on the device, it hummed with power. 'Well, it's working. I'd better go and find the Doctor, eh?'

'Affirmative! I shall wait here.'

Romana watched the Shadow move over to Astra. A claw-like hand plucked the control-cylinder from her throat. 'Now, my Princess, your work is almost done. Your destiny is at hand.'

Released from her trance, Princess Astra recoiled in horror at the sight of the Shadow's skull-like features. 'Who are you?'

The Shadow seemed to grow in menace until he filled the cave. 'I am the Shadow. The Shadow that accompanies you all!'

At the top of the tunnel, Drax paused as he heard the sound of approaching footsteps. He ducked down as the Doctor passed by, the giant mute close behind him.

Drax scrambled out of the hole and crept cautiously after them, stabiliser gun cradled in his arms.

The Doctor paused at the door of the TARDIS, and looked up into the skull-like face of the giant mute. 'When I give the Shadow the Key to Time, he'll kill me you know,' he said conversationally. 'Kill you too, I shouldn't wonder and all your fellows. He'll have no more use for you, will he?'

The mute said nothing.

Over the giant creature's shoulder, the Doctor saw Drax peering round the corner.

'Still, perhaps you don't really care,' the Doctor went on. 'Perhaps you're not really alive anyway!'

Drax crept nearer.

The mute forced the Doctor up to the door of the TARDIS, and gestured with his blaster.

The Doctor fumbled for his key, and opened the TARDIS door. Drax was very close now, with a chance for a clear shot at the mute. Why didn't he fire?

Suddenly Drax shouted, 'Right, Doctor, I'm ready for you!' He jumped forward, raised the stabiliser gun and fired—straight at the Doctor.

13

Small World

A glow of light bathed the Doctor's body. He became smaller, smaller, smaller ... until he seemed to disappear.

Immediately Drax swung the stabiliser gun round and fired at himself. He too, shrank, smaller, smaller, smaller, until he was gone.

The astonished mute looked down and saw two tiny figures scuttling across the floor. He raised his boot ...

The Doctor found himself haring across a floor that had suddenly become an endless rocky plain. A colossal black shape was crashing down on him ... The Doctor dodged frantically and the boot struck the rock floor with a thunderous crash.

The Doctor ran on. He heard a voice call 'Doctor! Doctor this way!'

Drax was beckoning him from a jagged archway—in fact, the Doctor realised, from a tiny crack in the wall.

The Doctor ran towards him. Suddenly there was a thunderous explosion and a blast of heat. The Doctor glanced up at the angry giant towering above him, and realised the mute was shooting down at him with his blaster. Dodging between the explosions, the Doctor dived into the crack and collapsed panting beside Drax.

'You shrunk the wrong one,' he gasped. 'Why didn't you shrink the mute?'

Drax slapped himself on the forehead. 'Never thought of it.'

'Well you should have—oh no!'

'What is it, Doctor?'

'I've done something even sillier—I've left the TARDIS door open!'

'Don't worry, mate. I'll pop out and create a diversion, you nip over and shut the door.'

'When I'm this size?'

'I see what you mean.' Drax contemplated the miniaturised stabilister gun. 'We can't go out there like this, 'cause he'll stamp on us—and we can't go back to normal size in here, 'cause there's no room. We'd just fill up the crack.'

The Doctor nodded. 'Like putty!'

'Do you mind? Well, we've got problems.'

'We certainly have!' The Doctor began ticking them off. 'The TARDIS door is open, so the Shadow can just walk in and take the Key to Time. The time loop must be stretched to breaking point by now —and if the countdown reaches zero up goes Atrios and Zeos and all.'

'Life presents a dismal picture, you might say.'

'You might indeed. Then there's the Marshal.'

'He's on our side is he?'

'No, he's in the time loop as well, trying to make a rocket attack on Zeos.' The Doctor sighed. 'I just hope Shapp and Merak managed to get back to Atrios ...'

*

The War Room was deserted—naturally enough, since the war was officially over. Shapp had dismissed all the technicians, and now he and Merak stood alone by the communications console. They looked like a pair of battle-scarred veterans. Merak's head was bandaged and he was leaning on a stick, while Shapp had his left arm in a sling.

He was speaking into the communicator. 'Atrian control to Marshal. Come in Marshal ...' There was no answer. 'It's useless. He either won't or can't answer us. And that time loop's not going to hold him back for ever, is it?'

Merak shook his head. 'Apparently it'll stretch and break eventually—unless the Doctor can get hold of the sixth segment—which is connected somehow with the Princess Astra.'

'But she denies all knowledge of it?'

'All conscious knowledge, yes. But if the knowledge is *unconscious*, implanted in some way, maybe it would show up in analysis.'

'The Princess isn't here,' Shapp pointed out.

'No—she's in the power of the Shadow. But her medical records are all stored in the computer!' Leaning on his stick, Merak hobbled over to the main computer terminal, and began punching up data.

Shapp resumed his attempt to contact the Marshal. Some considerable time later, Merak came back across the room. Shapp looked up. 'Did you find anything?'

'Nothing. I've made every possible check. Behavourial, physical, psychological. Nothing shows up. Astra's just the same as anyone else.'

'Apart from the fact that she happens to have been

born a Royal Princess!' said Shapp with ponderous humour.

'*What did you say?*'

'Astra's just the same as everyone else.'

'*Except for the fact that she happens to have been born a Princess!*' Merak's eyes were blazing with excitement. 'It's been staring us in the face!'

'What has?'

'The most obvious difference of all. Astra belongs to the Royal House of Atrios.' Merak hurried back to the computer terminal. 'I'm going to run a series of genetic tests. Astra may be more different than any of us could have imagined.'

So infectious was Merak's excitement that Shapp followed him to the computer. He watched for what seemed a very long time as Merak punched up data on the readout screen, studying the flow of symbols with fierce intensity. Finally Merak switched the computer over to print-out, and stood studying the sheafs of paper, his face grave. 'Yes ... it's just as I feared.'.

'What is?'

'There's a molecular anomaly buried in the structure of the House of Atrios, transmitted from one generation to the next, and now, finally, to Astra.'

Shapp gave him a look of utter bafflement. 'What does all that mean?'

'It means that Astra herself, her every living cell, is part of the Key to Time. Astra must be destroyed, to save us all!'

Merak's eyes were shining with tears. 'You see, Shapp? You see?' His voice broke and he turned and hobbled rapidly from the room.

Drax peered out of the crack, and ducked back, as an enormous boot thumped down close to his head. The mute was still patrolling the corridor.

'Well, Doctor, we've still got one thing in our favour.'

The Doctor gave him a look of surprise. 'We have?'

'Mobility. I mean if we're only this big we're as good as invisible. Except we can't move.'

The Doctor was still making plans. 'If the Shadow gets hold of the first five pieces, as he undoubtedly will, then it's up to us to get hold of the sixth!'

'You don't even know what it looks like,' argued Drax. 'I reckon you're banjaxed, old son. End of the road. Finito.'

The Doctor was thinking hard. 'The Shadow said I'd already seen it. It's something to do with Astra ... Let's see where the other end of this crack goes to, shall we?'

Drax nodded. 'Suppose so. Better than staying here and getting the boot.'

The screen in the Shadow's lair showed a close-up of the TARDIS.

The Shadow looked from Romana to Astra in triumphant satisfaction. 'You see? Your friend the Doctor has eluded me—but he has made his last mistake. The TARDIS door is open. The Key to Time is mine!'

His captives forgotten in his excitement, the Shadow

hurried away.

Romana said fiercely. 'If he thinks we're going to give up now ... Astra, we've got to get out of here.'

'My destiny is here, in this room. Not on Atrios, not on Zeos, but *here*.'

Romana seized her shoulders and shook her. 'Forget the Shadow, you're free of his control now. We've got to escape.'

'No, I must stay. I am the sixth Princess of the sixth dynasty of the Royal House of Atrios.'

'Very impressive, I'm sure,' said Romana sharply. 'Let's get out of here all the same, before the Shadow comes back.'

Astra shook her head. 'This is the time of my becoming ... my transcendence.'

'What are you talking about?'

Princess Astra smiled eerily. 'Metamorphosis.'

'What do you mean—metamorphosis.'

'My destiny is here!'

Suddenly Romana realised the appalling truth. 'The *sixth* Princess of the *sixth* dynasty of the *sixth* Royal House of Atrios! Princess Astra, listen to me, we've got to get you away from here. If we don't the Shadow will win after all!'

She tried to pull the resisting Astra from the room —and saw mutes with blasters standing on guard at the door.

The far end of the crack emerged into another corridor. Drax peered round getting his bearings, then fished out a crumpled map. 'Here we are then. Up there, there's your T junction. Right goes down to the dungeons, left there's a tunnel leading to the Shadow's lair—or there will be, once I get it finished. Still a few feet to go.'

'So there's a way into the Shadow's lair he doesn't know about?'

'Not till I get the tunnel finished,' said Drax gloomily. 'And a couple of midgets like us won't be much use with a pick and shovel!'

'If we can get K9 to help, we won't need a pick and shovel. Maybe we can still give the Shadow a surprise.'

Drax tapped the stabiliser-gun. 'Back to normal size then?'

'Not yet. Small is beautiful at the moment, Drax.

'Maybe so. But big is better though, innit?'

The Shadow swept along the corridors of his domain trailing a cloud of darkness behind him, until he reached the room that held the TARDIS. The baffled mute was still standing guard.

'At last,' breathed the Shadow. 'The moment I have waited for! Open the door!'

The mute swung the TARDIS door fully open. A flood of light spilled out into the corridor. The Shadow shrank back, wrapping his skull-like visage in his cloak. 'Too much light ...' he croaked. He tried to make himself go forward, like a man swimming against a strong current but the radiance coming from the TARDIS was too much for him.

The Shadow fell back and pointed a bony hand at the mute. 'You! Go inside and fetch me the Key. Hurry!'

The mute plunged inside the TARDIS. The Shadow waited impatiently. 'When the Key is mine, I shall dispel all light. Darkness and night alone shall reign!'

The mute emerged from the TARDIS carrying the partially-assembled Key to Time in his hands.

With a scream of triumph the Shadow snatched it from him and scurried back to his lair.

K9 stood patiently on the floor of Drax's workshop, towering over the tiny Doctor like a colossal statue. A side panel in his outer casing stood open.

The Doctor looked up at him. 'Everything all right K9?'

'Affirmative.'

'Remember, it's absolutely essential the Shadow thinks you're still under his control. That's why we've deactivated the control cylinder and put it back. So keep it simple and convincing, all right?'

'I shall report: The Doctor and Drax have been eliminated.'

'That's the idea. Now just test the blaster before you go.'

K9 extruded the nozzle of his blaster. 'Testing now!' He fired and a chunk of rock dropped from the wall.

There was a yell from the miniaturised Drax, who was already inside K9.

'Are you all right?' called the Doctor.

'Just about. The bit I'm sitting on gets hot!'

'Sit somewhere else then! Ready K9?'

'Affirmative!'

'Right!' Forward, then K9! You're on! The Doctor clambered inside K9 and the panel closed.

The Doctor groped his way through the darkness of K9's interior and perched on a circuit casing next to Drax.

'Smashing idea this, Doctor,' whispered Drax.

The Doctor smiled. 'Well, I can't really take all the credit. Did you ever hear about the Trojan Horse?'

K9 moved off with his tiny hidden passengers.

The Doctor's last desperate gamble had begun.

14

The Key to Time

Back on Atrios a mute stood guarding the entrance to the transmat booth. The Shadow wanted no more uninvited visitors to his domain.

A gold bracelet flashed through the air and landed at the mute's feet. He stooped to pick it up—and crashed to the floor beneath Merak's hurtling figure.

Merak snatched the blaster from the mute's hand and thrust it into the skull-like head. 'Into the cubicle.' The mute obeyed and Merak followed. There was a flash of light and Merak found himself in another cubicle, one giving onto a rocky tunnel.

He thrust the nozzle of the blaster into the mute's face. 'Is this the Shadow's planet? Tell me!'

The mute nodded.

Merak raised the blaster and smashed it down on the bony head. The mute crumpled and fell.

Dragging the body from the cubicle, Merak knelt and began stripping the black robe from the creature's body.

Dragging the skeleton-like remains of the mute into a side tunnel, Merak put on the robes ... covering his face with the hood. A procession of black-robed figures marched down the tunnel before him. The gaunt figure in the lead was carrying a glowing crystal.

Merak slipped out of hiding and joined the tail end of the procession.

The Shadow marched back into his lair, too exultant to notice that he had acquired an extra follower.

He placed the crystal on the specially prepared plinth and stepped back to admire it. 'The fulfilment of all I have waited for since eternity began!'

K9 and his miniaturised passengers came to the end of a long rocky tunnel. The tunnel ended in a solid wall of rock, behind which if Drax's calculations were correct, was the Shadow's lair.

K9 extruded his blaster. 'Prepare for blasting.' He opened fire, and the rock wall began melting away.

His gloating over, the Shadow turned to Astra. 'Come, Princess, it is time to fulfil your destiny.'

Astra moved forward towards the glowing Key to Time.

Romana tried to hold her back, but the bony hand of a mute gripped her arm, pulling her away.

Astra moved slowly forward. 'My destiny!'

'It is for this that you were born, Princess,' whispered the Shadow. 'The sixth child of the sixth generation of the sixth dynasty of Atrios. Born to be the sixth and final segment of the Key to Time!'

'I am ready,' said Astra softly. She stretched out her hands towards the Key to Time.'

The disguised Merak sprang forward. 'No!' he shouted. But it was too late.

As Astra's hands touched the crystal, her body

glowed with incandescent light. For a moment she seemed to burn like a flame and then the flame dwindled and shrank.

When the brightness faded Astra had vanished. Hovering in mid-air was a strangely shaped glowing crystal, the sixth and last segment of the Key to Time.

The Shadow reached out to grasp the crystal, there was a shattering crash, and K9 burst through the wall like a battering-ram.

The Shadow whirled round. 'What is this?'

'My apologies, Master.'

'You mechanical idiot—'

'There is an intruder here.'

The Shadow turned and saw Merak his hood thrown back, standing beside Romana. 'He is of no account. Where is the Doctor?'

'The Doctor and Drax have been eliminated.'

'Good! These two shall live—just long enough to witness my final triumph. Guard them!'

'Master!'

The Shadow reached out his bony hands and plucked the sixth segment from the air. Reverently he carried it over to the plinth in one hand, and took the Key to Time in the other.

'*Now* Master,' said K9 softly.

The panel in his side slid back and a tiny Doctor and a tiny Drax jumped out.

Romana was watching the Shadow in horror. 'If you destroy the time loop millions will die ...'

The Shadow chuckled. 'A small beginning ...'

The Doctor whispered. 'Reverse the stabiliser, Drax —now!'

Drax fired, the Doctor's body was bathed in light and he began to grow ...

Instantly Drax turned the gun on himself and fired again ...

The reversal was so rapid that the Doctor and Drax seemed to appear by magic. The Doctor sprang forward, snatched the Key to Time and the sixth segment from the Shadow's hands, and headed for the door. 'Quick, all of you, back to the TARDIS.'

The Doctor was gone, Romana haring after him, Merak and Drax close behind.

'You fools,' shrieked the Shadow. 'None can resist the power of darkness!' The Doctor and his friends were gone.

When they reached the tunnel that held the TARDIS, pursuing mutes were already close behind them.

'You and Romana go on, Doctor,' shouted Drax. 'Me and K9 will hold them off here.'

'How will you get out?'

'Transmat shaft. Now get going. I'll meet you in the computer room on Zeos! I know how to switch it off —I built in a fail-safe!'

The Doctor and Romana and Merak ran on.

K9 and Drax waited in ambush, meeting the pursuing mutes with a roar of blaster fire. The leaders fell, but there were more behind ...

The Doctor ran on down the tunnel and into the room, opened the TARDIS door and ushered Romana inside.

Merak hung back. 'I'm staying here, Doctor. I can help Drax and K9!' He turned and ran back down the tunnel.

The Doctor darted inside the TARDIS. A few minutes later there was a wheezing groaning sound and the TARDIS faded away.

Reverently the Doctor put the Key to Time back on its stand. Romana watched him, sadness in her face. 'We're murderers Doctor, do you realise?'

'It wasn't our idea to use the Royal House of Atrios as carriers of the sixth segment.'

'What happened to Astra was *our* fault. We're pawns, Doctor, being used to do the Guardian's dirty work.'

'I don't like it either—but it's done now. Set the co-ordinates for Zeos will you?'

'Is that all you can say,' said Romana bitterly. She looked at the sixth segment in the Doctor's hands. 'Astra was a living being once—now she's just a—component. No power should have the right to do that to people—not even a Guardian!'

'Romana, if we don't get to Zeos millions more people will die—and we really will be responsible. Have you forgotten the time loop?'

Romana hurried to the console. 'It must be down to the last second! Can't you put the new segment in?'

'The final assembly is a tricky job—there just isn't time. Zeos, Romana! We've got to switch off that computer.'

Thanks to Romana's skilful navigation, the TARDIS soon materialised in the computer room itself. The countdown clock was still repeating its endless sequence—but by now the sequence read 3, 2, 1 ... 3, 2, 1 ... 3, 2, 1 ... The time loop had shrunk to a few seconds.

Brandishing a pair of cutters from the TARDIS tool kit, the Doctor dashed across the room and buried his head inside the shattered pyramid.

Romana looked on anxiously.

Suddenly Drax shot into the room and skidded to a halt. He looked at the ruined pyramid and shook his head disapprovingly 'Here, what a mess?'

The Doctor popped his head out of the pyramid and yanked out two loops of cable, one red, one blue. 'Drax, don't just stand there! Which is the fail-safe? Is it one of these two?'

'Green!' yelled Drax. 'Cut the green.' He scratched his head. 'Hang on a minute, it might be the blue ... No, it's the green!'

The Doctor cut the blue.

The digital clock counted 2, 1, 0 ...

'I told you it was green!' yelled Drax.

Romana braced herself for the explosion.

Nothing happened.

Beaming the Doctor re-appeared from inside the pyramid. Drax gave him a reproachful look. 'Didn't have to make such a mess of it, did you?'

'Well, without your valuable help ... You took your time getting here didn't you? What happened?'

'Young Merak copped a head-graze from a blaster. We had to carry him. Slowed us down didn't it?'

'How is he?'

'He'll live. K9's looking after him outside.'

Suddenly Romana said, 'Doctor, what about the Marshal?'

'The Marshal?' said the Doctor. 'Good grief, the Marshal! Quick everyone, into the TARDIS!'

They dashed inside and the Doctor hurried to the console. 'What about Merak and K9, Doctor?' said Romana.

The Doctor ignored her. To Romana's surprise he

made no attempt to take off but went to a seldom used section of the many-sided control console. He made a number of fine adjustments and threw a main switch ... 'There, that ought to do it ...'

'Fire!' shouted the Marshal.

The pilot's finger pressed the button—just as the time-loop snapped. The rockets ignited and the deadly missiles streaked away from the ship.

The Marshal leaned back smiling. 'The moment of victory. Any second now my beautiful mushrooms will blossom and burst.

He leaned forward to stare out of the viewing port, and gave a gasp of astonishment. 'No, no!' he shrieked. 'It's the wrong target!'

The rockets struck—and the black asteroid, the Shadow's Planet of Evil, disintegrated into one enormous fireball.

In the limbo between the dimensions the wraith-like form of the Shadow hovered, dying. 'I have failed,' he whispered. 'The Doctor has the Key to Time. His task is accomplished.'

As his life ebbed away, the Shadow heard a deep, scornful voice.

'You whimpering wraith, your death, is encompassed in my designs. Now the Doctor shall release the Key to me, and chaos break upon the universe!'

With a last scream of rage and despair, the Shadow faded into nothingness.

The last flaming fragments of the Planet of Evil faded from the screen of the TARDIS scanner.

'Good shot, sir,' said the Doctor softly.

Romana stared at him. 'But Doctor, he hit the asteroid. He was aiming at Zeos! What did you do?'

'Oh, nothing really,' said the Doctor airily. 'Merely set up a deflective forcefield between the Marshal and Zeos. It bounced the missiles smack onto the asteroid.'

'Oh is that all? I thought you'd done something clever!'

'You might have told us,' said Drax reproachfully. 'We was expecting to get blasted into infinity.'

K9 appeared in the doorway. 'Affirmative!'

'Sorry about that——' The Doctor checked himself. 'What am I apologising for, I've just saved all your lives. Can I drop you anywhere, Drax?'

'No thanks. Think I'll take young Merak back to Atrios on the transmat. I've got a contract job on down there. Reconstruction, war damage and all that. Me and the Marshal.'

'You and the Marshal?' said Romana incredulously.

Drax nodded. 'Well, he'll be out of a job now, so I thought I might take him on!'

'When did you arrange all this?'

Drax grinned cheekily. 'About half an hour from now, I reckon!' He cast a brief envious glance at the Key to Time. 'If you ever want to get rid of that, Doctor, I'll make you a good offer!'

The Doctor smiled. 'I'll let you know! Goodbye, Drax.'

'Bye, bye all. Remember me to Gallifrey!'

'With a cheery wave the little man disappeared,

and the Doctor closed the TARDIS doors behind him.

Some considerable time later, Romana and K9 watched in reverent silence, as the Doctor completed the final assembly of the Key to Time. Working with immense concentration he had removed the decaying chronodyne crystal, replaced it with the real sixth segment and sealed and locked the whole together with the Tracer.

Now the work was complete and the Doctor placed the Key of Time on its pedestal.

He stared at it, his face rapt. 'There it is at last. The Key to Time!'

Romana looked uneasily at him. 'Hadn't we better be setting a course for Gallifrey, Doctor?'

'Gallifrey?' said the Doctor absently. 'Why Gallifrey?'

'That's where we're going isn't it? To give them the Key?'

'I don't think so.' The Doctor turned towards her. 'Do you realise, Romana, I have the power to do *anything* now, anything at all? Absolute power over every particle of the universe, as of this moment? Are you listening, Romana?'

'Yes, of course, Doctor.'

There was sudden menace in the Doctor's voice. 'Because if you're not, I can make you listen. I can do anything. As of this moment, there is no such thing as free will. There is only one will in the universe—mine! Because *I* have the Key to Time!'

Romana backed away. 'Doctor, are you all right?'

'What?' The Doctor shuddered and seemed to control himself with a mighty effort. Then he said gently,

'Yes, I'm all right, but supposing I wasn't? The way this thing makes me feel ... Well, I should be very worried if I was somebody else feeling like that? Do you understand?'

'Yes, Doctor, I understand. The sooner we hand that Key over to the Guardian the better!'

Suddenly the shutters of the TARDIS scanner screen opened of their own accord. A white robed, white bearded figure appeared on the screen. There was a benign smile on the wise old face.

'My congratulations, Doctor.'

Th Doctor bowed. 'Thank you, sir.'

'You have accomplished your task with admirable despatch. The universe has much to thank you for.'

'It was a pleasure, sir. Wasn't it, Romana?'

Romana was looking at the face in puzzlement. 'Doctor, that's not the President?'

'I can assume any shape or form I choose,' said the Guardian soothingly. 'I appeared to you in the shape of your President at the beginning of your quest, so as not to alarm you.'

'Remember who you're talking to, Romana,' said the Doctor reprovingly. 'I told you he wasn't just the President.'

'Sorry, Doctor.'

There was a tinge of impatience in the Guardian's voice. 'Since you now have the Key to Time, Doctor——'

'I have indeed,' interrupted the Doctor. He pointed to the great glowing crystal on its pedestal. 'Do you like it, sir?'

The Guardian smiled. 'Yes, Doctor, I think you could say I liked it!'

'We're terribly proud of it, aren't we Romana? What happens now, sir? You said at our first meeting that if the Key was assembled for a moment the Universe would stop, and you could restore the natural balance of good and evil throughout creation?'

The Guardian was definitely impatient now. 'Yes, Doctor, that is correct! Will you kindly release the Key into my keeping so that I may do so?'

The Doctor turned towards the Key. 'Key to Time, I command you—May I ask a question, sir?'

'Well, Doctor?'

'The Key to Time is already assembled, isn't it? Surely you can redress the balance now anyway?'

'Doctor I must *have* the Key—for safe keeping. It is awesomely powerful.'

'And mustn't fall into the wrong hands?' The Doctor nodded. 'Quite so! Key to Time——' He interrupted himself again. 'And what about the sixth segment, sir? You know it was an actual person the Princess Astra? If the Key is maintained in its present shape she will be imprisoned forever.'

'That is regrettable, of course, Doctor. But with the fate of the universe at risk, individuals become unimportant.'

'I suppose you're right, sir. Key to Time, I command you—*to stay exactly where you are and obey only me!*' The Doctor sprang to the TARDIS console, and flicked a whole battery of switches.

'Why have you activated the TARDIS defences?' thundered the Guardian.

'Can't be too careful, sir, can we? It would be a terrible tragedy for the Universe if I turned out to be colour blind—unable to tell the White Guardian from the Black!'

Romana clutched his arm. 'What do you mean, Doctor?'

He pointed to the scanner. 'Look at him!'

The face on the screen darkened, twisted, changed to a leering scowling demon, gibbering with rage.

'Don't you see?' said the Doctor. 'The White Guardian would never have such a callous disregard for human life. Nor would he want the Key to Time for himself.'

'Of course not,' said Romana slowly. 'He'd have used the Key and then dispersed it again, brought Princess Astra back to life.'

'Exactly. The Key's been re-assembled for some little time now. I imagine the real White Guardian has had all the time he needs.'

The evil figure on the screen shrieked, 'Doctor, you will die for this!'

The Doctor laughed. 'I think not. The Key to Time is still mine, remember. Rage all you like!'

'I will destroy you, Doctor,' hissed the malevolent voice. 'I will hurl every particle of your being to the furthest reaches of infinity!'

'I wish I could stay to chat,' said the Doctor cheerfully. 'Still, you know how it is. Places to go, people to see, things to do ... Romana?'

'Yes, Doctor.'

'Stand by at the console. When I give the word—dematerialise!'

Romana hurried to the console and the Doctor went over to the pedestal.

He stood for a moment staring into the heart of the

glowing crystal. 'Key to Time, I command you! When the TARDIS dematerialises, you will dis-assemble and scatter to the far corners of the cosmos.' The Doctor paused. 'All except the Princess Astra of course, she'd better go back to Atrios, and Merak. Ready, Romana?'

'Yes, Doctor!'

'Dematerialise!'

The TARDIS vanished, and for a moment the Key to Time hung glowing in space. Then it fragmented, five crystals disappearing into infinity, the sixth speeding towards Atrios—where Merak, dazed and wounded, awoke to find Princess Astra standing beside his hospital bed. He thought he was dreaming—until she leaned down and kissed him.

Some time later, with the TARDIS suspended somewhere in the space/time continuum, the Doctor looked up from the centre console.

'You've got to admit it, Romana, I do think of everything. Come and see!'

A small black box had been built into the centre of the console. Its top was studded with rows of flashing lights, and there was a handle on the side.

'What is it, Doctor?'

'It's called a randomiser.'

'I see. And where are we going now?'

'I've absolutely no idea,' said the Doctor proudly. 'That's the whole point, you see!'

'Doctor you have absolutely no sense of responsibility. You're capricious, arrogant, self-satisfied, irrational—and you don't even know where we're going!'

'Exactly! You see, if I know where we're going, the Black Guardian could know too. Hence the randomiser.'

'What does it do?'

'I've fitted it to the guidance system. It works on a very complex scientific principle known as pot luck. Now no one will know where we're going.' The Doctor pulled the handle, and lights on the box began flashing in a random sequence. 'Not even the Black Guardian.'

Romana looked at the flashing box, wondering what new adventures lay ahead of them. 'That's right, Doctor. Now no-one knows where we're going—not even us!'

If you enjoyed this book and would like to have information sent to you about other TARGET titles, write to the address below.

You will also receive:
A FREE TARGET BADGE!
Based on the TARGET BOOKS symbol — see front cover of this book — this attractive three-colour badge, pinned to your blazer-lapel or jumper, will excite the interest and comment of all your friends!

and you will be further entitled to:
FREE ENTRY INTO THE TARGET DRAW!
All you have to do is cut off the coupon below, write on it your name and address in *block capitals,* and pin it to your letter. Twice a year, in June, and December, coupons will be drawn 'from the hat' and the winner will receive a complete year's set of TARGET books.

Write to:

TARGET BOOKS
44 Hill Street
London W1X 8LB

cut here

Full name ....

Address...

....

....

Age.....................

PLEASE ENCLOSE A SELF-ADDRESSED STAMPED ENVELOPE WITH YOUR COUPON!